Emma Gibbens lives in West Sussex with her husband and daughter. She has always loved to write and her dream came true in 2014 when she wrote and published New Day.

Other books by Emma Gibbens

New Day

Dear Suzanne,
Enjoy Love
xx

Published by Completelynovel.com

ISBN: 9781849146746

@GibbensEmma

Acknowledgements

My thanks are to my husband once again for putting up with me disappearing of an evening to write, my daughter for bringing me back to normality, my mum for support and listening to my ideas, both my sister in laws for their support, my friend Laura for helping me believe in myself and for my readers.

PREGNANCY &

PILES

Emma Gibbens

"Oh my god I'm pregnant"

Ok so this is how we found out. We arrived home from our honeymoon and I was a few days late for my period. I didn't think much of it because I was a bit late the month before, but to put my mind at rest I did a test.

"Babe"

"yes"

"you know when I did that pregnancy test last month and there was only 1 line?"

"yes"

"Um, well this one has 2 lines"

"What? Where? Let me look at that...... it's very faint that second line, I think you need to do another one just to check, it's rather late in the day and they say its better in the morning as your wee has stuff in it".

So after that conversation I was left somewhat sad because Graham didn't seem to be over the moon, so for the next 12 hours I was irritable and bloody annoying. I was on forums all day checking to see how accurate these tests were.

I couldn't sleep so at 5am I couldn't wait anymore, I had to do another test, so off I went to the loo.

"Shit, oh my god, oh my god, oh my god" CONFIRMED yes indeed we are pregnant.

I composed myself as well as I could (I looked a little scary with my cave woman hair, black eyes and morning breath) went back to the bedroom and sat on the bed.

"Well?" Graham said with a very tired voice.

"We are going to have a baby" I burst into tears.

I can't explain the feeling when I told Graham it was so wonderful, it is the best feeling in the world to know you are creating a new little life.

"Oh my god, really? Bloody hell, so soon. We just got married. Shit, so you must have been pregnant before the wedding?"

I laughed until I cried again and thought to myself, "just like me when I was younger, never wanted to miss a party!"

So now what? It's 5.30am. Too early to call the doctor; they don't open until 8.30am. I think that's what I am supposed to do.

God It felt like a lifetime waiting for 8.30am to come around. I dialled the number very carefully, my heart was beating so fast I thought it was going to come out my chest.

"Hello you're through to the morning emergency surgery, how can I help you?"

"………."

"Hello? Hello anyone there?"

"Oh sorry, hi yes, I need to see a doctor I think, as I am pregnant I think and this is what I am meant to do I think?"

"Ok. We don't class this as an emergency so how far gone are you?"

"I don't know, I have never been pregnant before"

"Oh, is that you Jane?"

"Hi yes it is Cathy, please, please don't tell anyone it is still sinking in and we are not telling anyone"

"Of course I won't. I can't anyway, its confidential. Look I will book you in this morning at 9.45am ok, oh and congratulations you'll be an excellent mummy"

"Thanks" shit I'm going to be a Mum.

I went and repeated the whole conversation to Graham and said sorry to him because we weren't supposed to be telling anyone we know until 3 months, and Cathy is a family friend. Whoops!

So, it has been confirmed after working out my dates I should be about 5 weeks pregnant, but they have booked us in for a dating scan to be sure, so I'm going to meet this little person in 3 weeks.

Today I am feeling ridiculously tired, quite faint, and sick, and my boobs really hurt they are a tad hard. Also feels like puberty all over again! Just Googled 5 weeks pregnant and all the symptoms are normal and to have no fear I will be glowing soon. Yay.

WEEK 6

I have got to go back to work tomorrow after having three weeks off for our honeymoon.

I have got to remember NOT to tell anyone that I am pregnant.

Graham and I went for a walk with my Mum and Dad this morning up Kingly Vale. It is so weird knowing I am carrying their grandchild and they don't even know.

Oh my god, talk about the steepest hill we have just walked up, my poor aching body, why didn't Graham try and persuade my Dad not to keep going?

New Day

Back at work today told everyone about our honeymoon and how lovely England, Scotland and Wales are (sorry we didn't make it to you lot in Ireland). Everyone said they missed me (still had to make my own bloody tea though).

Anyway turned my laptop on, and it went nuts. PING PING PING PING PING 385 emails I couldn't understand why I still had so many, I told everyone I was away and that if anything needed doing to contact the support team we have! 1st email I opened was one from the Boss saying we had to be in London for 9am tomorrow, great early start for me! Welcome back to reality!

New Day

5am nice! Off I set for my meeting, 6am stuck on A3, 7am stuck on M25 and saw a pile up which was bloody nasty. It's scares me all this travelling I do now I am pregnant, it's not just me anymore I also have precious cargo on board! I need the toilet so bad, I knew I should have stopped at that garage before the A3, this is going to be a fun day!

New Day

Well, meeting was shit, all I could think about is what our baby will look like or if it will be a girl or boy. Also the fact I nearly wet myself and how lovely it was to go for that mammoth wee! I have been sick twice this morning so I called the boss to say I was feeling poorly and that I will work from home. Morning sickness is weird you kind of dry heave, a bit like a cat being sick you totally convince yourself you're going to be sick so you go to the loo and the loo smell hits you and blurrgghhhhh.

New Day

Been sick twice already this morning, I have also been for a wee 4 times in the night. I didn't even have a drink before bed? Is this normal?

I dragged myself to the office today and the first thing someone said to me was "god, you look dog rough, I know women let themselves go when they get married, but Jesus Jane"

"Sod Off" was my answer, and they did.

Still working through my emails, I got another 30 since last night? I got bored with my emails so I googled a few things and wish I hadn't as this is what I came across.

- During pregnancy, the average woman's uterus expands up to five hundred times its normal self? OH MY GOD REALLY?

- Tall women are more likely to conceive twins? So I am 5 foot 8 inches so I consider myself to be tall, so now I am in panic mode does this mean we are having twins? I am going to have to ring Graham that we are having twins, shit I am going to have 2 babies.

- The number in multiple birth has increased by more than 400 percent, (I am now really scared does this mean I'm having triplets?) That's enough internet for me, I am going to throw up for the 3rd time and then go and eat my lunch.

New Day

Ok, so I have now expressed my concerns to Graham re having twins or even triplets. He said to me that I am being silly and that we don't have any twins in either of our families so stop scaring him and myself. I still don't feel any more at ease, the

internet is full of facts isn't it? It is quite scary not knowing what my body will do next.
I have been sick quite a bit today, I weighed myself I have lost nearly 7lbs in under 2 weeks? This isn't right, surely I am supposed to be putting on weight?

New Day

I am so poorly, I have thrown up so much, I have called my boss and told him I think I have a bug and will keep him posted. Graham said to call him if I need anything. This makes me feel a bit better. Graham is very sweet and understanding at the times I need him most. I went back to sleep at around 10am woke up, threw up, back to sleep woke up at 1pm threw up, ate lunch, threw up went back to bed woke up at 4.30pm threw up, cooked dinner for 6pm, ate dinner with Graham threw that up, Graham made me go back to bed and rest he said he would do everything for me. I must have missed this part out in the pregnancy books about how shit you can feel!
People say you are meant to have a glow about you! Well I don't, I look old, grey and skinny!

WEEK 7

I can't stop crying, everything is setting me off. I woke up and found out that we had run out of milk so I cried. I went to get dressed and the shirt I wanted to wear had a stain on it so I cried. Graham said I looked knackered so I cried. I even started crying watching a bloody mobile phone advert!

Apparently this is normal for 7 weeks, I googled it so I have warned Graham that my changing level of hormones will make me an emotional rollercoaster.

New Day

I am getting worried now as people at work keep texting me asking if I am ok, and my boss called me today and said he is getting asked by lots of people saying they are concerned because I am looking thin and ill! I burst into tears because I am supposed to be glowing except I am melting! I am only 7 weeks pregnant but Graham has said I have got to tell my boss as I can't keep going off with a sickness bug and he hates the fact I drive over 200miles some days. So I called my boss and told him, he was really happy for me and Graham and has promised not to say anything until I am ready to tell anyone. Great so now our old family friend knows and my boss!

New Day

So we told my Mum and Dad today that they are going to be Grandparents. They are so made up. We had to tell them early because I am so poorly, I keep making excuses why I can't eat or drink things and I have been off work a lot. I have never seen my mum and dad look so proud of me before apart from my wedding day, it is a picture I will never ever forget. I am so glad Mum knows now, as I can confide in her, ask her about all my symptoms and share this time with her, because without my mum I wouldn't be here to have my own baby. Wow, I am getting all emotional writing todays diary.

New Day

So now I am back into the swing of things at work and have nearly caught up with my emails. Just got to the last one and it's about a meeting in Cannock 306 miles away, great better get the sick bags ready. What I have never understood about my work, they always hold the meetings in Cannock, because it's apparently central to everyone! Most of us live in or near the South Coast! (I am sure it has nothing to do with the fact 3 of the bosses live in Birmingham).

New Day

Jesus my boobs are really sore, I can't even run they hurt that much. Graham tried copping a feel this morning but he just copped a slap from me instead.

I went to make some breakfast this morning, opened the fridge and oh my god that smell (I had to run to the loo to be sick which really hurt my boobs as I was retching so much). I returned back to the fridge with a scarf wrapped around my head and face and emptied most of the fridge into the bin.

“Honey, where’s my blueberries?”

“In the bin”

“Ok, where’s the raspberries?”

“In the bin”

“Ok, where’s the strawberries?”

“In the bin”

“Why?”

“They stink I can’t have them in there.”

“They were all new packs of fruit, they couldn’t be off already”?

“They stink and make me heave”

“Ok”

After a very sorry looking breakfast Graham came into the bedroom and sprayed his aftershave all over himself.

“Oh my god that stinks, you can’t wear that anymore, I think I am going to be sick”

“Ok, I am going to work now and I will get some breakfast on route and I will also stop off at the shops to get you some cotton wool to put up your nose so you can’t smell anything, bye love you

WEEK 8

So far I have been married about 6 weeks and I am 8 weeks pregnant, my poor husband has really had to obey the sickness and in health vow! He has had to cook for himself as I am always sick with the smells, he has had to put up with me crying most days and he has had to put up with me being really moody. Bless him he really is a lovely man, not many men would hold their partners hair back for them to throw up especially when it can be about 7 times a day and all hours!

New Day

I got a phone call this morning from my father in law at 7.45am about his neighbours. Why do old people wake up so early? They are foreign (and all I can say he is not the most politest of people, I would say he is bordering on embarrassingly rude) and they had a party in the garden on Saturday night, so instead of any normal human just knocking on their door and asking them to be a bit quieter, he started lobbing shingle across the fence into their garden, and in the morning at 7am he banged on their door and read them the riot act. They didn't understand so he pushed his way through into their lounge, turned on their computer and typed it into google and translated it into their language and then they understood. Apparently they are friends now, but he wanted to tell me in case I heard a different story! I don't care, I have my own issues I don't need to listen to this!

New Day

Graham called me today, said he was worried about me as he has seen I've been on ebay looking for a commode. I explained to him that I keep needing the toilet which is really disturbing me at night and that I have nearly wet myself. He told me to stop being dramatic. Dramatic?! I have a baby growing inside me which at some point I will have to push out and he says I am being dramatic? Well hell yes I am, I think I have a right, until he has a vagina and a womb I think he should keep his opinions to himself, oh yes and he said I am really aggressive at the moment, whatever!

New Day

We told Jack (my stepson) today that we were expecting a little sister or brother for him and he said he already knew! Apparently he worked it out as I had stopped drinking wine at weekends (bloody cheek), I had sold a lot of my beautiful high heel shoes on ebay and that I have been wearing baggy clothes. He did seem happy though which means a lot to me.

New Day

So I have arrived at Cannock for this bloody meeting, I have been sick 3 times in the car and I feel like shit. The hardest thing is, I have to put on a brave face as I can't tell anyone at the moment! I am so concerned that I am harming our baby where I keep being sick, I called Graham when I got to my room and cried. He is booking me in to see the doctor. I hope baby is ok.

Had a shower and got ready for dinner with all my colleagues, met up in the bar and everyone was ordering alcohol. Scott asked me if I was having red or white I said "water please". Bugger me I got a bit of a reaction from that! Everyone was on my case "go on have a bloody drink, let your hair down" I just said I couldn't as I was training for a race and that alcohol was forbidden. Scott knows me very well and just threw me a look as if to say are you pregnant!

Saved by the bell, my boss announced that dinner was in 10 minutes and to make our way down to the dining room (I am so tired it is 8pm I am usually in bed by now). I was not looking forward to this at all, 3 courses. I started with the mushrooms, so far so good kept it down which is a bonus. Main course Lamb Shanks, oh my god it was the size of a small dog. I took one bite it was greasy and chewy and oh shit I am going to be sick, legged it to the toilets and threw up everywhere. On my return I hid most of it in a napkin, how no one saw me is beyond me. I couldn't face pudding and again Scott threw me that look of "I know you're pregnant!" It was 10pm when everyone finished and some bright spark said "let's go to the bar". So we all walked to the bar which was closed (there is a god). I sneaked off to my room, threw up 2 more times, I hope I am ok in this meeting tomorrow.

New Day

Breakfast smelt rank, I couldn't stomach it, but I had to have something so no one (Scott) would suss.

The meeting was so boring, all I could think about is what our baby will look like, if it will be a boy or girl, how big it is at the moment and of course if they are ok from all my throwing up! Everyone must think I have a bowel or bladder problem as I had to get up to go to the toilet to throw up about 5 times in 3 hours.

Meeting finished at 4.30pm which meant I arrived home at 9.45pm, I walked in like a zombie, muttered a few words to Graham and then collapsed into bed. Graham came into the bedroom and tucked me in and rubbed my feet until I feel asleep, total heaven.

WEEK 9

Went to my best friend Sarah's house today for a spot of lunch. I have a thing for salt and vinegar Hula Hoops filled with Cheese and avocado (how no one at work has sussed yet is beyond me). I couldn't believe what happened it was like the end of the world.

"What the bloody hell is that?" I said

"What?" She said

"This"

"What"?

"This" I pointed at the black rotten avocado.

"Oh dear" she said

"Oh dear? Oh dear? What the hell am I going to do now" I just burst into tears grabbed my car keys and drove to not 1, not 2 but 3 different shops to buy an avocado. Apparently I overreacted!

New Day

I texted Sarah this morning to apologise for my behaviour yesterday lunch time. Looking back now I did overreact. Being pregnant is dangerous, we should be locked up, I didn't realise that cravings would take over my body and brain like this. I have another craving which is Cox Apples, BUT, they have to be really cold (about 12 hours in the fridge). Of all the cravings I could have had, my body chose apples! Before I became pregnant I always said to my pregnant friends when I have a baby I am going to have cravings like cake or chocolate well basically anything bad for you. I didn't realise you couldn't choose!

New Day

Wowsers my boobs have grown over night, I swear to it. I woke Graham up and showed him my boobs, he looked delighted, and he told me not to get dressed as this is a rare scene for him at the moment! I must admit I look bloody sexy, I look like one of those glamour models, slim, big boobs and a happy looking man in bed. I told Graham I was going to get some new bras to fit my new boobs and he said he would help. We both had different ideas. He showed me, basically, a prostitute outfit, and I showed him my nans outfit (that's what he called it). I think the moment passed for Graham after that!

New Day

Called Mum today to ask her if it is normal to go to the loo all the time like 40 times a day. Mum has confirmed says it's normal.

WEEK 10

Ok so I really can't stop being sick, anything I eat or drink is just coming back up. I have been signed off for 2 weeks at work. I feel so, so ill I am so worried I am harming the baby. I have no bump yet and I am getting so skinny, my mum said you can see my spine, where in all them fucking pregnancy books does it say any of this. NONE! I am so scared, I phoned my mum to come round as Graham was at work. I phoned the NHS helpline and they told me to get my Mum to bring me down to the hospital to get checked out, so off we went. I was attached to a drip as soon as I arrived as I was severely dehydrated. After being in for 5 hours (my poor mum) they sent me home with Anti sickness pills that people take for travelling on boats, they are safe to take when pregnant!

New Day

I have been sick twice already and its only 9am. My best friend Sarah came over today who is about 8 months pregnant and she told me that she woke up the other night to her boyfriend asleep on the other side of the room on the floor. She asked him why and he replied "you kept farting in your sleep and it got a bit smelly". She said she could have died she was so embarrassed. I am now really worried because being a newlywed and not farting yet in front of Graham (I am very lady like in this kind of area). Apparently you can get very gassy when pregnant!

New Day

Called mum today and asked her if its normal I can't go for a poo, she has confirmed it is normal during pregnancy. I went onto the internet to see why this is the case and apparently your hormones cause the smooth muscles of your large bowel to get sluggish causing constipation. I need to eat more whole grains and vegetables. Great, I bet I get piles!

New Day

I got out of the bath today and caught site of my naked body and I had a mild heart attack as my body from my neck to my lady bits are covered in blue veins. I called my midwife as I was near on looking like a Smurf and was a bit concerned. She reassured me that it is a healthy sign that my body is working and that it is a motorway of blood supply to my new baby. They will disappear after baby is born. She also told me that I will be noticing all sorts of changes to my body from large boobs, to a line down the middle of me and maybe stretch marks which are all very normal and common. Great!

New Day

I feel so poorly again today I just have no energy what so ever, the tablets are working but sometimes the tablets just aren't up to the job. I am getting so upset hearing other mums talk about how they love being pregnant and it is such a wonderful feeling because I have not experienced this yet. I wish I could tell everyone I am pregnant and that I have terrible morning sickness (well all day sickness).

WEEK 11

Graham and I went to hospital today to have the 12 week scan (even though I am 11 weeks they would not have been able to see me until I was 13 weeks and I couldn't wait). We were so excited we got there early so we decided to go and get a tea from the machine (why do they make the cups out of thin card so you get 3rd degree burns holding them). When we were waiting to be called in there were some misfits sitting opposite us, they stank of cigarettes and looked like they needed a good wash and the language coming out of their mouths made your skin crawl, I felt a bit vulnerable. Anyway the nurse called out a ladies name and to our shock this he/she beast thing with its crack hanging out of its trousers, tea stain down its top, stubble, deep voice and hair you could fry an egg on stood up and walked into this room. Graham said that whoever got that pregnant must have been drunk, paid or blind. Now, I know people say it is the personality that counts, and it's what inside that really matters, but surely it does have something to do with looks, because take the elephant man for instance, he may have had a brilliant sense of humour but he didn't have them queuing up did he?

The scan was amazing I cried (happy tears) so much seeing this little person that we have made. I was told I was not allowed to go to the loo and that I had to drink 2 pints of water beforehand as it is easier for them to see the baby, oh my god when she put the jelly on my belly (that just made me laugh writing that) and then pushed down HARD I might add onto my bladder, I thought I was going to wet myself. We got to keep 4 pictures so we donated £5.00 to the hospital baby unit. I can't wait to show my Mum and Dad. They are going to be so happy.

New Day

Ok, so not only do I keep throwing up, I am now getting severe heartburn and the stomach acid is bloody awful. I have found that Gaviscon is my new best friend, I drink it like it's going out of fashion. Graham says I look like a secret alcoholic as I keep going to different cupboards and taking swigs from the bottles I have placed all over the flat! I phoned my midwife today to see if it is normal to get heartburn at this stage and she has assured me it's normal, I bet she laughs about my pathetic phone calls to the other midwives.

New Day

I came across a website today saying that my baby's fingers and toes are now fully formed and that they will kick but I won't feel it yet, it also said I should stop feeling sick now hahaha do me a favour! Who writes these websites? A man?!

WEEK 12

Ok so the time is 3am and I swear I can feel my umbilical cord being pulled? I want to wake Graham and tell him, but he will just think I am being silly. So I poke my belly every time baby tugs it. At least I am not the only one awake.

New Day

I went to the doctors as I was concerned with this strange feeling and he reassured me that its normal. The reason I can feel this is because my baby is playing with the cord and will be tugging it like a rope and this will make me feel like my belly button is about to fold inside its self! Great so now I have Tarzan growing inside of me!

New Day

I am so, so, so happy today. My book "New Day" has been proof read and edited, and went live on amazon today. I cried so much seeing it on there, let's hope that it does well and can fund my year off looking after baby, because the government won't as I don't qualify. This is so bloody annoying. Why don't I qualify? I have worked since I was 13 so surely I have put enough into this greedy government.

New Day

I can't stop yawning. I think I am turning slowly into a sloth. People must think I am so rude I just yawn constantly, it must look like they bore me! I really do hope I start feeling better soon, I only seem to feel normal when I am asleep, so I suppose I'd better just go back to bed!

New Day

I swear I have got more hair on my body now I am pregnant. I read in all these pregnancy books that when you're pregnant the hair on your head grows faster and thicker, which is true, but I was not told that I would also turn into a silver back monkey. I have quite a lot of hair growing on my belly. My poor husband, not only have I stopped shaving my legs as I can't be bothered, I now have a hairy belly! God I am turning into that beast from the hospital having its scan.

WEEK 13

So I woke up today and saw that I am showing quite a bit now even though I am only 13 weeks, so we have decided that I can now tell everyone at work. So now I can explain why I have been off a lot, and that is from morning sickness, touch wood though the last couple of days I have been feeling so much better looks like the tablets are working at last. So I arrived at work and announced it to everyone and they were all so happy for us, it was so lovely seeing people's reactions. My 3 closest friends at work cried (happy tears), which set me off again! Most of the men I work with said "you lucky cow, wish I could get pregnant and have a year off, you woman have it so easy". (I kept my thought to myself, oh its real easy having a period once a month, giving birth and menopause) I just laughed. It is such a relief to have told everyone now.

New Day

Why is it when you are pregnant people start to treat you as though you have a disability? I mean, don't get me wrong, I love people holding doors open for me, letting me get the lift first, getting the comfy seats in cafes and being let through to the front of the queue when shopping, but when I am out with friends for lunch, they start reading what they have on offer to eat, and read it to me - I'm pregnant not blind! Then they take the tray from me as though I can't carry it - I'm pregnant I have not lost my arms! Then they sit me down and order for me, I'm pregnant not a bloody child! I am not even half way through my pregnancy, God knows what they are going to be like when I am about to pop.

New Day

One thing Graham and I have noticed since becoming pregnant is the fact I swear a lot more, I rang my Mum and asked her if this is normal, she said it's not a symptom but it is normal for me to swear (bloody cheek).

New Day

What is that saying "when you're pregnant you bloom and glow?" It's bollocks. Don't believe it. I have been sick for almost 9 weeks, I have high blood pressure and I have got a pile because I am so constipated it is unreal. I am going to look like a sack of shit by the end of my pregnancy.

New Day

Seeing my book on Amazon and knowing family, friends and my twitter followers are buying it makes me so proud. I cry when I see reviews and when I see my book creeping up the list, I can't thank Graham enough for making me finish my book and getting it out there.

WEEK 14

So at work today at around 1pm I was at a loose end (to be fair to myself I had done all my work as I had been up since 5am being sick so I went to the office early). So I went onto google and typed in strangest laws from around the world. (I have no idea why I chose to google this but I am glad I did).

Apparently in England it is illegal to die in the houses of parliament. I'm not sure if this is true but if it is, you wouldn't really give a shit as you're dead so it's not like you will go to prison is it?

Also, a pregnant woman can legally relieve herself anywhere she wants even in a policemen's helmet? Now I won't be trying this because I'm not sure this is true and if it isn't then I really don't want to go to prison.

Apparently in Logan County, Colorado, kissing a woman whilst she is asleep is illegal. (How the hell would the women know that he kissed her whilst sleeping? It's not as if he would confess to then be prosecuted is it!

Apparently in Alexandria, Minnesota, having garlic or onions on your breath means you legally CAN'T have sex with your wife. If this is true I am 100% behind this being brought into England. I can't stand smelly breath in sex especially now I am pregnant!

Apparently in Alabama you are breaking the law if you are in control of a motor vehicle if wearing a blind fold! Why would you do that anyway?!

I do have to laugh. Two of the office juniors just walked past my office and one said to the other "She is always busy, I would hate her job" if only they knew!

New Day

Called mum today to see if it is normal to feel really sleepy all the time. Mum confirmed it's normal.

New Day

I'm getting so forgetful at the moment, so I have bought a pack of post it notes and they are everywhere, in the house, in the car, in my office. I thought baby brain was after you had the baby not before? I will have to google this.

New Day

No need to panic I'm not going mad apparently I am in the "FOG" stage of the pregnancy!

New Day

Scott at work today said that he will miss me when I have gone as I make him laugh, bless him. He also called me a bitch as I have a year off. I did remind him it's not an actual holiday. I do have to give birth and then look after a person who can't do anything. He still thinks I am lucky. He thinks I won't come back to work; I reminded him that money does not grow on trees and that I will have to come back to work (it's so depressing to know I have to come back to work, I could say so much about people claiming but I won't as they are not all the same)!

WEEK 15

At last I am now actually now enjoying my pregnancy. I have stopped being sick so much (I am typically in the minority having such bad morning sickness). I am also so excited that we have our 20 week scan soon and we are finding out if it is a boy or girl. Graham is worried about us finding out as he has said once we know I will be off shopping. He said it's so nice that the bank statements are clear from all the clothes shops I shop in every week and that we have never had so much cash hahahahaha.

I went to the post office this afternoon and found myself rubbing my tummy. I always said I never understood why pregnant women did this, but now I know it is the most relaxing and normal thing to do and that is to love your baby and to make sure they are safe.

New Day

I got on the scales today and I have put on only a little bit of weight. My boobs are massively amazing, I can't stop touching them and looking at them, no wonder all these glamour girls get them out. They are one perk of being pregnant! I am again feeling very happy.

New Day

If men got pregnant I bet morning sickness would be the number one health problem of the world, but because its women it is just sickness!

New Day

Called mum today to ask if it's normal that my boobs look fake and have gone up 2 cup sizes in a few weeks. Mum has confirmed its normal.

New Day

I was sitting at my desk when I overheard two of my colleagues talking about what they had for dinner last night and this is how the conversation went.

"I had sea bream last night for dinner, it was actually really nice but it did taste really fishy"

"Really? I would have thought it would have tasted more like chicken flakes"

Now I was left confused as of course it will taste of fish - it is fish. What the hell is chicken flakes? And these two women work in accounts and look after a lot of money!

WEEK 16

I got a random phone call today from another company wanting me to work for them, how gutted am I? He (the man on the phone) wouldn't give me a chance to speak. (That's a first) "Hi Jane, hope your well? It's been a while since we last spoke, but I have got a company who wants to meet with you, to discuss a Senior Manager role based in East Sussex, 48k a year basic plus up to 20k bonus, car, laptop, phone, and office how does that sound?"

"Lovely, but I am 16 weeks pregnant"

"Oh dear, really? That's a shame. Shall I remove you from our data base, it's not like you will be working again?"

I just burst into tears and put the phone down, how dare he speak to me like I was a worthless piece of shit when I told him I was pregnant! My life is not over. It is just beginning. How bloody dare he. I emailed Graham to tell him what had happened and his reply was "well, you're not as young as you used to be and once you're a mum you are not as appealing to the career world". I burst into tears again, god my hormones are all over the place at the moment.

New Day

My stepson went out tonight and I didn't think much of it until it got to 1am and he was still out. I remember my mum saying to me that I gave her nightmares wondering where I had been on nights out, strolling in at all hours and to wait until I have kids then I would understand. Well now I know what she means, he strolled in at 6am. Once he returned I fell asleep only to then be woken up by the bloody dustmen at 7.15am!

New Day

So my cravings are all over the place, I googled what my cravings mean and I came across a website that said beetles taste like apples, wasps taste like pine nuts and worms taste like fried bacon. Well that's most of my cravings so I'm sorted if the shops run out of my food. I might apply for a survival weekend with Bear Grylls after I have had baby.

New Day

Maternity pay at work is crap. All I get is 90% of my pay for the first 6 weeks, then statutory pay for the rest of the 9 months which is about £123.00 per week and I am now worried, as I earn this in a day, how the hell will we survive? How is it fair I get the same pay out from the government as someone who has never worked? I think it should be like for like, you should get your normal pay as long as you return to work. I suppose I won't be buying clothes and shoes for myself for a while, so that's a big saving there and I won't be having my nails done any more so that's a huge saving also. I really can't see myself blooming, all I see in the mirror is a cross between Worzal Gummidge and Grotbags and I just want to cry.

New Day

Graham took me out for lunch today as I have been feeling really low lately (hormones I think). Whilst we were waiting for the waitress to take our order, a man came in and asked a man behind the bar if he could book a table for 12 people at 7pm tonight, the waiter said "sorry sir, bookings that large need to be made 24 hours before so our catering team can prepare and we would need to have taken a £50.00 deposit" the customer replied "oh really? Ok well can I book 2 tables for 6 people next to each other then?" the waiter then replied "Sure, can I take your name" We couldn't stop laughing I mean how bloody stupid is that!

New Day

I was doing a spot of research on my pregnancy and when my baby should arrive etc. this is what I found out.

Your first baby is usually late which is true, about 62% arrive after their due date, 35% early and only 3% on their actual due date. The timing is tied closely to the length of your monthly cycle, if is shorter you're more than likely to give birth early, if your monthly cycle is longer then you will most likely be overdue but if it is usually 28 days between each cycle you will more or less deliver on the due date. So I have re-read this statement at least 30 times and I still have no clue what it is trying to explain. I thought the way I explained things dragged on, but this is something else!

WEEK 17

I have woken up with a blocked nose and I am constipated – great. Llooks like I need to up the fruit and fibre and remember not to strain going to the toilet, the last thing I need is another Farmer Giles!! I phoned Graham to get him to stop off at the shop on the way home to grab all sorts of fruit and veg and explained my constipation to him. I could have died, he had me on loud speaker in the office!

New Day

I am really worried that I have blown my nose too hard and strained too much going to the toilet as I have veins all over my boobs, arms and belly all of a sudden. So I called Graham at work. He just laughed at me and said it's all symptoms of pregnancy and the reason my bowel movements have slowed down is because the hormones progesterone slows it down (he said this with a very confident smile I could tell by his voice) . I didn't believe him. I thought he was just trying to get rid of me so I googled it and he is right, he must be researching pregnancy and reading the book I got him!

New Day

Bloody work is doing my head in, I went into the office at 7am to catch up on my paperwork as I couldn't sleep. I turned on my laptop and it took 20 minutes for the bloody thing to load up. I put my password in and it failed, so I typed in another password and it failed, typed in another one and it failed. I started to panic a bit at this point as it was my last attempt before it would lock me out and the only way back in is to call IT which are useless and don't start until 9am which was 1 and a half hours away. So I had one last try and I did it, I was in. PING, PING, PING, PING, PING, PING 76 emails, I closed my laptop and went to make a coffee. I share my office with a couple of people and a guy called Michael ,who is definitely going through a midlife crisis, as he has started to wear shiny suits with surf beads round his neck. He says things like "radical" and "sure thing dude" and has been looking at convertibles! Anyway, I walked in and he said to me "God, you look like shit". I just burst into tears and he panicked and started being really nice and asked if I was going to tell our Human Resources department what he just said. This made me laugh and snot flew out of my nose in the process. He was too kind to say it landed on him, so he just said he would go and make us a drink (I bet he went into the kitchen and disinfected his shoulder where my snot had landed, how embarrassing). Now I have an office pet, I will draw up a list of things I need doing, otherwise a trip to our Human Resources department!

New Day

Called mum today to see if it's normal to eat loads of different random food, mum has confirmed its normal and it is especially normal for me as I have always eaten random different food! (bloody cheek).

New Day

I was watching "This Morning" this morning and decided to text in to win one of the prizes as it only cost 50 pence and your normal network charge to have a go at winning a bloody nice car and £36,000. I know I won't win, I never bloody win anything. I used to buy Take a Break magazine and entered every week, because someone in my home town was in it as they won, so I thought I had a chance but never won. I even entered online surveys to win money to spend in their stores but no, I never won. What's that saying "you have got to be in it to win it?" Bollocks!

New Day

I now find myself looking at new mums and their babies, I hope they don't think I am a weirdo. I do find myself bloating my stomach out more and rubbing it to show I am in fact pregnant myself and not some crazy lady!

WEEK 18

I have been getting serious heartburn lately, so I have been drinking a lot of peppermint tea and eating smaller meals which is really hard for me as I could eat a trough full of food, every breakfast, lunch and dinner. In fact all day long I could just pour food into my mouth. Why the hell am I so hungry? I think I am going to need to get a barrel of Gaviscon on repeat prescription. The plus side to this is, I have got over morning sickness and putting weight back on.

New Day

Went to the doctors and they have prescribed me with Gaviscon, not quite a barrel size but its free as I'm now entitled to a free NHS Card as I'm pregnant - what a bonus. I feel like an alcoholic swigging this stuff, it really does work though it's amazing. I can't stand the mint one, it reminds me of the early stages of pregnancy when I went to brush my teeth and the taste of toothpaste would make me gag until I was sick! I like, no I mean I love, the aniseed flavoured one. It is amazing.

New Day

I went to the doctors for my midwife appointment and I heard our beautiful baby's heart beat for the first time today. I cried. It is the most beautiful sound in the world, to think Graham and I have made this little person who is now growing inside me. I asked the midwife to keep the sound on whilst I recorded it to send to everyone on my phone. I could have listened to that heart beat forever, I didn't want her to stop it.

New Day

I got on the scales today, I have gained 12lbs already? That is almost a stone, but I am still only a size 10? My mum said it's because I lost so much at the start being poorly, so I am just putting on the weight I lost. Graham said that it is my boobs as they are now an impressive 38DD, and he is not complaining. We love my new boobs!

New Day

In my pregnancy book it says that our baby should be around 14cm long and can suck their thumb. How lovely is that, also I read that if I had a scan now it should be apparent on the ultra sound picture what the sex of the baby will be as organs are already developing. Baby girls will be developing eggs in their ovaries already (that's mad to think if I am carrying a girl I am also carrying my future grandchild)!

New Day

I called mum today to see if it is normal to breathe like a heavy smoker, mum confirmed it is normal.

WEEK 19

I want our baby now, work is so hard at the moment, I can't concentrate at all. I have to travel loads and I hate it, I really hate it. People can't see you're pregnant when you are driving I feel so vulnerable. It has made me realise how many bullies there are on the motor way. I don't know how I am going to fit behind the steering wheel when I get bigger. I have to have a risk assessment at 25 weeks so I will have to see what happens then.

New Day

Graham is pissing me off today, he has been a bit ill and he hates work at the moment so of course it is all my fault! I asked him what he wanted for lunch and he said cheese on toast, so I went to the kitchen to make it. When it was ready I took it to him and he said "what's that?" in a really annoying moody childlike voice. "Cheese on toast, toasties how you always make them" I replied. He threw himself out of bed like a stroppy teenager, "that's not what I asked for" chucked it in the bin and redone himself a load more cheese on toast. He is in such a mood I can't stand him like, this it is so unattractive and makes me feel like a totally worthless prat. I stormed off round to my mums.

New Day

Called mum today to thank her for letting me sound off yesterday and she said not to be silly. I will have plenty more of those days to come!

New Day

Whenever I get comfy and settle down the baby goes absolutely nuts. I get kicked and punched until I move around again. I wouldn't mind so much, but when I am stuck in traffic on the M25 it is very uncomfortable. The one good thing about travelling now is that I have someone with me now I can talk to without looking crazy. Mind you, people still think I am crazy as they won't see that I am pregnant. I have got to stop swearing so much also, as I was told that baby can hear my voice.

New Day

I was in Costa today waiting for my friend on one of the two comfy sofas by the window, and whilst sitting waiting some old man made a very loud remark about how fat lazy people who don't work take all the comfy seats that should be for him, he has paid his taxes all his life blah, blah, blah and caused a bit of a scene. Usually I would have started shouting abuse back at him, but since being pregnant I have been able to control these feelings and deal with situations a lot differently. I got up and stood face to face with him (bump stopped me from actually being nose to nose but I was close) and said "firstly I am not FAT I am Pregnant, secondly I am not LAZY I have a job and work bloody hard, thirdly I am waiting for my friends to arrive and, lastly, I am waiting for my coffee that I paid for with the money I earned. So the next time you open that old mouth of yours think about it first, because it may not be someone as nice as me confronting you, comprendez?" With this he scurried off to the back and a few mums and grans clapped, I felt like a little celebrity hahahahaha. Reading this back I do sound like I may still be a bit aggressive?

New Day

Graham and I have been talking about where we could move to, and one of the places is Canada due to him loving snowboarding and the fact it looks so beautiful. I told mum and she made out she is 100% behind us but I know that she would hate it. Then I told dad and he told me I was being ridiculous and that it is obviously my hormones making me think stupid ideas. I don't know if I could actually do it and take their grandchild away from them. Graham said that Canada is just like England was 50 years ago (I don't know how he knows this he is only just 40 himself) anyway all this talk was making baby summersault in my belly, Graham said baby is practicing snowboarding!

New Day

I am so out of breath at the moment, I only need to walk about 5 steps and I am done in. I called Graham to see if we could get a stair lift put in at home. He put the phone down on me. I think that may have meant a no.

Apparently at 19 weeks you should be planning your maternity leave, I was really shocked when I read this as I planned mine the day I found out I was pregnant.

WEEK 20

I can't believe that I am half way through my pregnancy already. It is so amazing my beautiful baby will be here soon and we find out this week if we are having a girl or a boy. I hope I don't blow off when they put that cold gel on my belly because anything that is cold, or pressure on my belly causes me to blow off as I have no control over it. I went to the dentist today to have a check-up. Why, when they put that sucker thing in your mouth to dry it out does your tongue decide to attack it, even though you are telling your brain to keep your tongue well away from it? It's so embarrassing.

New Day

I played a poker tournament this evening for my husband as he was at some seminar thing to do with his work. I was very proud of myself I came 3rd out of 1500 people and I won £139.00 so that's going towards a new buggy. It was so funny as there were 5 of us left in this tournament and the 3 with the most chips (I was one of them) bullied the other 2 so we would all win something. I was trying to type in the chat box at the bottom of the screen and tried to type their lingo but I came across way too girly and had to come clean, that in fact I was not my husband, I was actually his wife. I automatically got respect from the lads which gave me so much confidence that I am now considering becoming a professional poker player!

New Day

I was lying in the bath tonight and Graham came in to moan about how shit his day had been (great relaxing bath this has turned out to be). In mid-sentence the bath water rippled, so he burst into laughter and made fun of me blowing off. I assured him that I had not blown off but then it happened again, which set Graham off again. It happened 3 more times and every time the water rippled I felt movement in my belly, it must have been baby telling Daddy to stop moaning.

New Day

Oh my god we found out today we are having a girl, I cried and cried happy tears. I think Graham cried worried tears knowing I was going to start shopping straight away.

When we were having the scan the lady said “she is looking healthy, oh you did want to know the sex didn’t you?” and that is how we found out, just like that. I called my mum and dad first who were over the moon, and then everyone in my phonebook got either a call or text.

I asked Graham if we could pop into Next on the way home to see if they had any baby clothes we could pick up, Graham just ignored me and we went home.

New Day

So I have been shopping and I have spent a fortune, I have bought so many beautiful outfits that I would even wear them if they were in my size. I wonder if when she is older she will look at photos of her and curse me for dressing her in some of the outfits. I remember the Velcro trainers and shell suits I was made to wear as a child.

New Day

My mum told me that when we lived in Redhill Surrey, her and her friends every week would take a 40 minute walk with us babies to a clothes shop called Quality Seconds just to browse, and every now and then they would buy something and this was the highlight of their week. She also told me that when I was a baby I only had 5 outfits and 5 sleep suits and that was enough. She said that already I have enough to clothe about 20 baby girls, I just can't help it though. I just see more and more beautiful clothes and I just have to have them.

WEEK 21

I went to Sarah's today and whilst I was there a neighbour came over and started talking about what I should and shouldn't eat whilst being pregnant. Peanuts came up and she went mad when I said that I eat peanuts and peanut butter. She said I could kill my unborn child blah, blah, blah so I flew of the handle at this remark and demanded evidence of such a ridiculous statement, she had none apart from knowing a nurse. Well bloody hell don't we all know a nurse? I told her she was being pathetic and that she was wrong to say such a nasty thing to me, she then flew back at me and said what if your baby is allergic to peanuts, I then flew back at her (god we sound like birds with all this flying) well she could be allergic to milk, butter, bread, meat or vegetables but I wouldn't stop eating all that because I would then be ill making her ill. I hate people who think they know it all.

New Day

I'm so fed up today at work because everyone is talking about what they are doing this weekend, they are either going shopping for new clothes, or going out for a drink, or going for a long walk in the woods and going for a pub lunch and pint, or going off surfing or just having fun. I can't do any of these things it feels like I have been pregnant for years and I still have 19 weeks to go. I swear baby knows what time of day it is, she is so wriggly around any feeding time and quiet around bedtime. But I have found that at 3am she decides to do summersaults and keeps me awake for an hour or so.

New Day

I rang my phone banking account today and asked them to check something for me as I couldn't get online as their system was down, so they asked me some security questions. First they asked for my mother's maiden name but not the whole name, they say a number I say the letter. I passed the first one, the second, the third but I failed the forth and they said "sorry but we can't accept it as you said the same letter and you have already used it" I replied "I know because 3 and 4 are the same?"

The woman on the other end again said "sorry I can't accept that" I replied "why not? It's my mother's maiden name you have to except it" Like a bloody robot she repeated "sorry I can't accept it" I told her she was a jobs worth in my pregnant way (not very nicely).

I put the phone down and phoned my local branch who sorted it out in minutes.

New Day

Why is it when us women become pregnant or have children we think we know what's best and turn into Doctors? I keep diagnosing my friends children and discussing with Graham how I would deal with the situations if I was in them. For instance, a colleague of mine has sent her two children to school with chesty coughs and I wouldn't have. I would keep them at home in bed drinking lemon and honey drinks and eating chicken soup all day, it worked for me as a kid. Honestly I think I could be a doctor with my knowledge of the common cold, croup, nits, constipation, sleeping problems, bed wetting and the gammy eye (not sure this is the technical term). I have read so many books on all these things, as I am so sure that our child, at one stage, will get one or a couple of these.

New Day

I went to a baby sale near my mums today. It is like an inside car boot just for babies and young children's stuff. It is amazing, it is full of all sorts of people from your hard grafters, mums who have never worked, chavs and grandmas. I bought so much stuff, in fact I bought 4 bags worth. I couldn't believe it, I bought 5 brand new with tags baby-grows all 20p each. I also grabbed a bargain of a French Connection Dress with tags for £8.00 the rest was all from Next and Monsoon. I must have got about £150 worth for £30. I always said I would never buy used stuff, but do you know what, I have and I am glad. I like to call it "pre-loved".

It is fantastic as it saves you loads of money, it is basically new as they grow so fast they are not in it long enough, and if I don't use it for my baby I can always sell it on. I can't wait for the next sale.

New Day

I read that if your mother had an easy pregnancy and delivery then so will you, well I am well and truly screwed. I was a little cow (my choice words not my mother's) when I was born I came out legs first so they had to cut my mum 4 ways to get me out, she also had a team of doctors and nurses (about 12 all in all) watching as it was quiet rare to see this when in training. I think I am going to go for a cry and a lie down.

WEEK 22

I burst into tears today at work and my sidekick Scott didn't have a clue what to do (bless men) he just sat there and let me blurt it all out.

"How will we cope, me not earning" I sob.

"Why would it affect me?" Scott says

"What? Oh shut up Scott, not you and I, me and Graham, it's going to be so hard, I don't know how we will do it, we will have to sell everything and live in a shed in my parent's garden".

"Jane I think you are being a tad extreme there, I don't think you will end up in a shed"

"Being a bit extreme? It's the bloody truth, I'm going to have to breast feed the baby for all its life it cost £10 for formula which works out around £250 for 6months worth, in fact I will have to breast feed Graham and myself, that is enough money to pay for a month's council tax and the electric, oh god I need to call Graham and tell him to sell the house and start looking for a shed".

So I called Graham and there was no answer, so I left him a tearful message about how we are going to be homeless. Scott, bless him, slipped out of the office whilst I was on the phone and made me a decaf coffee and got me a jammy doughnut. He really is my best mate at work, I honestly don't know how I would get through the day without him. He is just like a brother and a sister in one, as he looks out for me and also has the best bitch fest conversations about people at work.

New Day

I'm never ever eating chilli sauce again. I have had the runs today and my bum is on fire. I have used so much Sudocream (reminds me I need to buy some for baby).

I seriously am not enjoying this, I have to sit right next to the bathroom as I can't move as quick as I could when it was just me I was lugging around, I don't want an accident, I think I might look into getting a commode again.

New Day

Is it child abuse if I make my baby kick stuff off my belly? She is really good at it she sent my mobile flying the other day, but she struggled with the television remote as it is quite heavy!

New Day

I tried to sit up and get out of bed this morning for a wee, and I couldn't I was like a tortoise on its back, Graham had to help me do some sort of roll and rock movement to budge me. I still have 18 weeks left of this, I am either going to have to sleep standing up or hire a crane in!

New Day

I woke up today feeling really energetic, less aches and pains and my boobs look massive - I love them! I may have put on some weight (18lbs so far) but hey I have big boobs so I don't care. If I wasn't pregnant I would be worried, but all my friends who are mums say it is normal and it falls off you after you give birth so I'm going to treat myself to a dirty fat double chocolate cake to celebrate this exciting news.

New Day

I googled what stage our baby is at and what it is doing, and it said that our baby can hear me when I talk, so I sing to her now and she wriggles about. I am not sure if she is dancing or trying to get away from the howling noise I am making. My mum bought us a book for the baby. You are supposed to read it to the bump to get used to your voices. So I have arranged for Graham and I to have story time every night at 8pm, so we all chill out and listen to each other.

WEEK 23

Wow. I woke up this morning and I am looking BIG. Baby must have grown loads last night I think I will lay off of sausage and mash for dinner! I saw the John Lewis advert on Television today and it made me sob so much. Graham asked if I was alright, and I told him about this advert and he just laughed at me, so I cried even more. Baby is really active today I think she is going to be a dancer, Graham thinks she will be a triathlete!

New Day

There are certain things I can talk to Graham about that is about my pregnancy and there are certain things I can't. For example my best friend Sarah has had children so she knows most symptoms of pregnancy. So when I asked her why my knickers look like I have sneezed in them and showed her she didn't flinch, pull a face or throw up. She just answered me and said "this is a totally normal symptom of mid pregnancy but if it is thick and yellow call your midwife just to check it is all ok" and I was happy with this diagnosis and stopped worrying. However Grahams reaction was totally different to Sarah's, he flinched, pulled a constipated face and nearly threw up and said to me "that's disgusting, surely that's not normal, why would you tell me that let alone show me, I think you need to see a doctor that is not normal" his reaction worried me which made me ask Sarah.

New Day

Oh my dear god I have seen it all now. An old lady just left the supermarket (I am sitting in the café by the window) and actually stopped in the pouring rain talking to herself and clicking her car key at a car and it not opening. After 3 minutes (I timed her) of trying to get into this car she realised that this actually was not her car. So she was walking up to all the cars the same colour pointing her key fob at them until she found her car. This old lady has just pulled away in her car (well I hope its hers) in the wrong gear and bunny hopped out of the car parking space into her trolley she forgot to put back and then drove off the wrong way to the exit (one way system). This is another reason why I believe you should have to take your driving test again when your over 70!

New Day

Lara at work was telling me that when she was near her due date she wanted to go into labour and she had heard somewhere that if you have sex this can happen. Her husband was mortified she wanted sex at such a late stage in her pregnancy and said it just wouldn't feel right, she had a massive strop and said she will never sleep with him again when baby is born, so he gave in. So for three nights on the trot nothing was happening. Baby was well and truly staying inside Lara, so she told her midwife what was happening and she asked Lara if she used a condom, to which Lara said yes and her midwife laughed and said that's the reason why it probably has had no effect as it is the sperm that makes the labour come on. When she explained this to her husband he was so upset and said that he felt used. He flatly refused sex with her until baby was born, Lara said it was hilarious as their baby didn't come until 2 weeks after that episode, and he was so eager to have sex again she became pregnant for a second time shortly after!

New Day

I was sitting in a garden centre café in Surrey and was people watching as usual. I saw an old couple and I couldn't quite make out what this old man was saying to his wife, but it sounded like he was putting her down on everything she suggested. When he got up to get their coffee she took a deep breath looked up and closed her eyes for about 7 seconds (I timed her) and I thought that poor woman in her 70's (I hope she doesn't drive) has probably put up with him for years moaning and putting her down. He had a face like a slapped arse, turned down mouth and a really scabby looking fox shaped face and she looked frail and fed up. I just wanted to cuddle her and tell her it will all be ok. She really did look so lost and sunken. Do people in unhappy relationships just get to a point and think oh well, I might as well carry on as I have put up with it for years? I would hate to be that unhappy. People need to get a grip, you get one life so bloody live it.

New Day

My fact of the day is the word QUEUE this is the only Word in the English language that is still pronounced the same way when the last four letters are removed.

WEEK 24

I keep walking into things today, I am walking like I am drunk. I'm really not having a good day at all, I am sweating loads so I keep stripping off. I hate work at the moment. All I want to do is potter about at home and talk to bump instead of listening to customers moaning about crap. Everyone at work is so depressing at the moment they are all bitching about one another and then lovely to their faces, then they all moan about their jobs and how they hate the place. I just want to shout to them "WELL FUCKING LEAVE THEN, MOVE ON OR JUST SHUT UP", but I don't. I just smile at them knowing I have just bitched about them all to bump. I really can't wait to leave for maternity and take a year out. It will be so nice not to have to troll through 60+ emails a day and try to communicate with incompetent people, I think I need to go back to bed and wake up again!

I am also devastated that I have, in fact, piles. Why the hell did I have to get them? I called my doctor and he wants me in to check to see if I need cream. How embarrassing, and yes, I have now been prescribed Anasol! I handed over the prescription to the chemist sticking out my bump so they knew I was pregnant and that is the cause of them. I have been told to drink more water and eat more roughage to help soften my poo! Oh praise the lord I have NEVER EVER felt so embarrassed and unattractive in all of my life. (Fancy calling it Anasol).

New Day

So I have decided to go to a place called Home Sense near me. They do lovely stuff for your home and as I have a week off from work (yay) I decided to do a spot of shopping. Now that I am pregnant I park on the end spaces to give me room to get bump and I out of the car safely. I spent £180 on cushions, crockery, towels, a chair and a few bits for baby. Got back to my car and some fat bastard has parked so close to my car that not even a stick man could get in the car! I know that they are fat as the hand print left on my car looks like the hand print of Shrek. Why do people who own those pickups go bloody shopping in them? They don't fit in spaces. Drive a normal car if you're out shopping! I stormed into the shop and asked them to put an announcement out but no one came so I wrote a shitty letter saying "*You clearly need to lay off the pies as your hands look swollen. If you insist on driving a wagon that big, go park it in the ditch, oh, and you may want to visit a garage on the way home. I accidently kicked your car several times trying to get into mine. Have a nice day ☺*". I then got in my car from the other side and drove off. NEVER PISS OFF A PREGNANT WOMAN.

New Day

My best friend has just had her baby, she is so adorable I can't wait for our babies to meet. It means so much to me I can share these precious times with her, she is like a sister. I would do anything for her and when we both found out we would be having a baby so near together it was such a special moment. Her other little girl was playing in her bedroom whilst we were in the lounge, and she wandered in touching her chest saying that they hurt. She was wincing, then a pair of breast pads fell out of her vest, she then picked up her dolly and pretended to breast feed. After about 10 seconds she asked her mum for nipple cream as her nipples were sore from all this breast feeding. It was so funny, yet scared the living daylights out of me as I will soon be doing this, and oh my god breast pads are awful. They look like circular sanitary towels.

New Day

I am starting to feel like an elephant as I keep thinking I can squeeze passed things then realising I am stuck half way. I am so ready to pack up work now as I am so tired and finding it really hard to hold in my wee when I'm on the motorway (bloody M25 car park). I will need another risk assessment soon as I am sure this can't be right? I was walking to a café that is on the industrial estate my work depot is on, and I was wearing my new fitted black maternity dress. It was very flattering and perfect for my hot flushes as it keeps me cool; anyway I was walking along and I hear a whistle and a beep shouting something obscene about getting something out for the lads (you can't tell I am pregnant from behind). So when I turned round to see where all this commotion was coming from, two lads in a scaffolding lorry looked mortified when they clocked my tummy. It made my day - bloody idiots!

New Day

Every morning before Graham leaves for work he whistles to baby and sings through my belly, it is so sweet but as soon as he has left the house she kicks the crap out of me. I think she's doing this to me because she wants daddy to carry on or to punish me for allowing Graham to do it. I bet that she is going to always whistle, I just hope it is in tune unlike Graham!

New Day

I have had a really low day at work today. Everyone is doing their own thing and organising stuff without me. When I asked Scott my sidekick why, he just said "because you're pregnant and you won't be overly active and you won't be able to come on these events". I just cried and cried and cried. The poor sod didn't know what to do. It dawned on me today that in 16 weeks I am going to be a mum, I have got to give birth, it won't be just Graham and I anymore and this scares me, it really does. Don't get me wrong, I can't wait to have our baby, but I'm going to have to seriously grow up!

I did cheer up in the evening though, as Graham was laying his head on my tummy listening to baby move around and all of a sudden she kicked out really hard at his head, so he kept putting his hand in different places and pushed back and she would kick that area. They did this for about 25 minutes, it is the most beautiful thing to watch. I think she is going to be a daddy's girl.

WEEK 25

I have ordered a long body pillow as I can't sleep very well at the moment, my bump is getting very heavy and it makes my hips ache. So at the moment I have about 6 pillows around me, poor Graham can't get a look in at the moment.

New Day

DON'T TOUCH ME! God I'm so irritable. The thought of anything or anyone touching me makes me want to scream, so I have phoned work and told them I'm not coming in as I think I have a viral infection or something. I called midwife and all is ok, "it's a symptom of pregnancy, no panic". Bonus, so now I have a day off. I called Graham and he came home early as he thought his luck was in. DON'T TOUCH ME!

New Day

I had my risk assessment at work done today. Worked out bloody brilliantly. I am not allowed to travel anymore as the motorways I drive on do not have toilets on them and I would 99% of the time get caught in traffic, and I am not allowed to sit in a car for any length of time. The only down side to this is that I am now office bound and I hate being office bound.

New Day

My pillow arrived! Graham and I are so happy, I get to cuddle a pillow and be comfy. Graham gets his side of the bed back, his pillows and he also gets to cuddle me. I can't wait for bed time now.

New Day

So bored today I went on a bloody Health and Safety course for work, of all the things to be teaching me! I hate this course so much. I am leaving soon and will be off for a year, so I don't see the point in me doing it? I did try and get out of it but NO, company policy states I have to go on it!

These courses are nonsense, we have the most useless trainers (our company spent over 1 million pounds on this lot of trainers, we would rather have all got a pay rise and worked a bit harder). You don't learn much and you get a certificate at the end stating you are competent Health and Safety risk assessors! (God help the customers that let us go out and risk assess their places). We were going through the risk assessment part and the trainer filled it in wrong and said not to worry as no one looks at them anyway! It's madness really, but hey, I don't care. I now have a certificate stating I am competent in Health and Safety!

All day after the course I just pissed everyone off, stating why the fire door shouldn't be propped open with a box, cups of tea should not be left by plug sockets and electrical equipment, and that they must all wear hi-vis jackets outside in the car park at all times. I love pissing them off because I know I am leaving soon.

New Day

So today I have decided to pack my overnight bag for hospital. I have packed knickers, bras, nighties (donated by my neighbour as she said I will need a few it could get messy), socks, a book, bathroom stuff, a towel, and bits for baby like nappies, baby grows, blankets, hats and gloves. I have repacked it about 20 times adding things and taking things out. Graham asked why I was packing it now so early, and I said because I could give birth anytime from now. He nearly fainted, panicked a bit and googled if this was true. It's true. Poor Graham.

WEEK 26

My car is going into the garage to be re-sprayed this week so we can sell it. We want it to look nice and shiny for the pictures to go onto Ebay and Auto Trader. We are buying a caravan because I want one, and the rest is going towards Graham's business venture. It is all so exciting we have decided to set up a furniture business all made here in West Sussex, England designed by Graham. I have never seen him so excited.

New Day

Whilst I was at work I got a phone call from my step son just letting me know that some old man has just crashed into my parked car trying to reverse into a space that a ferry could have backed into! He took pictures of the man and his car, and, him even getting out of his car and touching mine trying to rub the marks off of it, then driving off. I just cried when I saw the photos, we are supposed to be selling the car. Graham and I both drove home and called the police. They said there is nothing they can do as the witness is my stepson and that means he can't be my witness. I cry again and called the policeman a heartless prat and put the phone down. Graham decided to take me out for a walk to calm me down and said we will pass all the information to the insurance company and they will sort it all out for us. We just got round the corner and there it was, the heap of shit that crashed into my car. Graham run home got a pen and paper and wrote a note to stick on his windscreen.

"We have a video and pictures of you ruining our car with your superb parking skills, you'd better call me on my mobile (left number). P.s my paintwork that has been left on your car looks good maybe you should re-spray your car that colour!"

New Day

So I have decided today with Graham, that I want a water birth, after watching One Born Every Minute. It looks the quickest and least painful. He laughed at me when I said this and said "we'll see".

I have started to get a brownish line down the centre of my belly to my lady bits, apparently this will fade after I have given birth, I quite like it if I am honest , it is sweet. I am rubbing in oil to all my wobbly bits, hoping and praying I won't get any stretch marks. So far so good.

New Day

I called my mum today to see if it was normal to get really clumsy during pregnancy. It's normal. Apparently it gets worse after you have had the baby, I am slightly worried about this.

New Day

Work is so boring at the moment as I am not really doing much anymore as my job role has changed a lot! I am doing all the admin for the people in my team, I hate it, they keep piling more and more on to me as they know once I am gone they will have to start doing it again.

I wish I was giving birth already! Get me away from this hell hole.

It is amazing though how crap some of my colleagues are at their paperwork and to think some of them are getting paid more than me!

WEEK 27

So today Graham and I went to a really pretty town called Midhurst to see a shop we were enquiring about to set up the furniture business. It looks a bit on the small side but it's quite cheap and a really good location, we had about 20 minutes to spare before we met with the agent so we took a stroll through the town and about 7 shops down there was a furniture shop identical to what we wanted to do. It had a massive sign in the window saying "we are closing down tomorrow". We both looked at each other and have both decided that we will have to rethink our business adventure... back to the drawing board.

New Day

I phoned in sick again today as I couldn't bare being at work, I have had the worst nightmares about babies dying and it has kept me awake all night. I was so glad Lara at work answered the phone, she just told me to take off as much time as I needed. So I have thought about it and I have decided to take the whole week off. The midwife came over today and said I should be putting on around 1lb per week from now on but no more as this could cause stretch marks around your tummy, hips and thighs. I don't mean to sound thick, but when you get a craving for something, you have got to eat it, so if it means I put on 2lbs or 3lbs a week then so be it. I am eating for 2 right? I am however concerned about this because it means I will be putting another stone on top of what I have already put on!

New Day

God what is wrong with me? I woke up crying and then woke Graham up to have a go at him for cheating on me with some woman from the Co-Op! He told me to stop being so silly and to go back to sleep, but I couldn't so I went into the lounge to watch Along came Polly on dvd, and woke up about 7am I couldn't remember for the life of me what part I got to. Graham came in with a decaf tea and apologised for cheating on me in my dream. I burst into tears because I am convinced he will leave me, because since we have been married I have been really ill, pregnant, not wanting sex, crying, moody, fat and fussy with my food. He reassures me that he isn't going to and that he meant his words "in sickness and in health, death do us part" I love my Graham.

New Day

Just had a phone call from my garage. It will cost £3000 to fix my car to get it back to what it previously looked like before the titanic smashed into it! Why are old people allowed to drive? The DVLA should take his sodding licence away from him.

New Day

I went round to see my neighbour today. She has a son who is autistic and he can only say a few words in a sentence and the first thing he did when he saw me was point, prod and poke me saying 1.2.3

babies! He thinks my breasts are babies. Great, I knew they had grown but that's a bloody joke. They are a 38F at the moment which is pretty big, but the fact it looks like I have 3 children hanging off my front is very distressing for me.

New Day

Good god I am eating so much today. Scott at work asked me if I wanted anything to eat from Greggs bakery so I said I would waddle down with him for exercise (Graham has told me I need to keep active as it is important to both myself and baby). It would normally take 5 minutes to walk there but I have slowed right down and it took around 10 minutes. This has made me even more hungry so when we arrived I picked up the following 1 ham salad roll, a bag of cheese and onion crisps, 1 yumyum doughnut, 1 cherry bakewell tart, 1 sparkling water and a bag of quavers just in case the cheese and onion was not enough. When I got to the counter to pay the lady looked me up and down and said "all for you love?" I burst into tears and she immediately apologised and felt really bad. They gave me a pack of extra yumyums to say sorry. BONUS.

WEEK 28

Ouch it really hurts, I think I have broken my hips. Graham had to call the midwife today as I really couldn't move my back or my hips. I got stuck in bed at 3am and nearly wet myself. Graham had to carry well drag me (I am too heavy now) to the toilet. My midwife came out to assess me and has diagnosed me with SPD (I thought this was some sexual disease and immediately thought about Graham and that co-op dream). She explained to me that SPD actually stands for Symphysis Pubis Dysfunction, and I have been referred to the hospital for physio. I also brought to my midwifes attention that I think my lungs have collapsed as I can't breathe properly. She assured me that they haven't and that it is just my diaphragm is compressed by my growing uterus! I can honestly say being pregnant is not fun, it is not glamorous and it makes you feel and look like a bloody hairy Walrus (your husbands or boyfriends who tell you otherwise are bloody lying).

New Day

I went to ASDA with my neighbour who also has children and we wanted to go to the baby event to grab a few bargains. I spent £80.00 which was well worth what I purchased as I now have enough wipes and nappies to last baby until she is about 2 years old. I bought a changing mat, sponges, soaps, a mobile for the nursery, a bouncy chair, a teddy, a glow bug for her room and some baby grows. I don't normally go to ASDA as it is about 40 minutes away from where I live and I am a Waitrose girl through and through. Anyway, we were looking at the baby Johnson's starter kits (they are bloody brilliant) and there were these two girls I can only describe as overweight chavs, swearing and burping and making a scene and one of them said to the other "swear down babe, over ere, these fuckin Johnson fings, 25 quid down to a fiva, but fuck that, I aint goin to part with my dollar, I know it's cheap but it aint cheap enuff. I can't nick it as I'm already on a caution so I've hid one, so when I pick up my giro I can get it and hopefully it will go down even more in price". I really feel sorry for her unborn child, I really do.

New Day

Graham loves spooning me and bubba. I love it to and I know bubba does. I know this because when Graham falls asleep he twitches, and bubbas response is to kick me. It is so sweet but I am starting to feel a bit like a punch bag.

New Day

I could have punched Michael at work today, he told my boss he thinks I am too fragile and not cut out for the job anymore as I keep crying. I went mental and told him what a jumped up little prick he is and that everybody is saying that he is going through a midlife crises. No-one under the age of 40 in this company fancies him and they think that he is, in fact, a creep. Everybody who was in the office at the time laughed and cheered when he walked out of the room. He said this to my boss after he witnessed me crying after a Chinese customer rang me to ask where their order was and they were shouting and getting angry at me. But looking back now they were not, in fact, shouting or getting angry. They just spoke like this to be clear, as they couldn't understand the contract. Oh my hormones are everywhere at the moment.

New Day

I got a call from H.R today telling me that I was lucky Michael didn't log a complaint against me yesterday! How dare they? He was the one who bloody started all this, he was lucky I didn't log a complaint against him. After that phone call I went to make a drink and I had to pass wind which I have been a lot (apparently this is normal at this stage in your pregnancy, this is what I have been telling Graham anyway) so I did a quick rekey of the area and let one go. It made me laugh as it sounded like a bee stuck in the systems cupboard at work. When I walked back into the office with my tea, the I.T guy (I think his name is Colin) asked me if I heard any strange noises coming from the system. Someone had just told him that when they were walking past the kitchen area they heard a buzzing sound coming from it like a bee. (How bloody embarrassing) I am not sure if they are taking the mick because they knew I had let rip in the kitchen or that they really believe there is a problem with the system?!

New Day

I called mum today and just cried, she said this is totally normal. I think my mum is probably thinking I only call her now just to check on my symptoms, I never ask how she is feeling or how dad is, so maybe I need to call her. I really don't know what I would do without my Mum and Dad.

New Day

Today I decided to wash all the clothes I have bought for baby when she arrives. I am so lucky my neighbour and best friend have given me bags of clothes. Looking at all the clothes drying made me so excited-it is getting so real now. My last wash was a dark wash, so I threw in one of Grahams pride and joy Lamb's wool jumper, 40 minutes later. SHIT. Looks like baby has a new jumper, I rang Graham and confessed to him what I had done and then just cried. When Graham got home, he showed me a beautiful bunch of flowers he got me.

WEEK 29

My midwife told me today that I should be wearing my glasses instead of my contact lenses now as my eyes will start to dry up, as the moisture in your eyes alters when you're pregnant. I did google this as I didn't believe her and she was correct. My boobs are hurting so much, I sent Graham out to buy me some new pregnancy bras and they are hideous. They look like two igloos stuck on a strap and they fit on his head (yes Graham did actually try my bra on his head and took a picture). I still have no stretch marks I'm so lucky, keeping my fingers crossed. I love the oil I am using from Boots I swear by it, it is amazing and half the price of the leading brand for pregnant woman. I am so keen to look for a yoga class for pregnant woman, but I know deep down I won't bother going even if I find one, I am so lazy at the moment it is unreal. Graham has told me to rest as much as possible because I will need all my energy when bubba comes along. It is my birthday soon and I am supposed to be excited as it is my 30th but I am finding it hard as I was not expecting to be 29 weeks pregnant, This means I can't drink alcohol, I can't go clubbing, I can't eat seafood, basically I can't do anything.

New Day

Graham has told me that for my 30th we are going to France and I cry (happy tears for once). It will be our first time away together abroad. We have been told we will not be able to fly due to me being pregnant, so this means we will have to drive which now means we can't go to the South of France as I am not allowed to be in the car for that long so we are going to the North of France and I can't bloody wait.

New Day

So we are all packed and ready to go to France, we are going on the Euro Tunnel. I am so excited that every 10 minutes I have been going to the toilet (this has concerned Graham as he doesn't want to have to keep pulling over for me to have a wee). I have bought a couple of French books to learn a few words so we fit in a bit better. I practiced a couple of phrases on Graham and he laughed. He said I sounded like Boycie from only fools and horses, so I have decided to not bother. So when we arrived in France, Graham asked me to navigate as he was driving (oh dear). Graham took the wrong turning (he blames me and I cry, it probably was my fault but he was driving faster than I could keep up) which meant 8 toll bridges later (30 euros poorer) and 100 miles extra to our journey we arrived at our beautiful B&B. We did argue when we arrived because as Graham pointed out we could have actually gone to the South of France with that extra detour. Anyway we checked in and went straight up to our room and the smell of fresh paint hit us. It was so strong it must have just been done (great now I will get a headache), we went to put the kettle on and realised they didn't have one (I cried) and you had to order them at 3.65 Euros each! We decided to freshen up and I was already to have a relaxing bath and Graham had to tell me there was only a shower (I cried). The shower was good though very powerful and bubba liked the water hitting my belly.

We went down for dinner and we ordered Duck with Frites, they came back over and put a bottle of Tomato ketchup on our table-just our table. When they returned I asked why and they said "you are not English no? All you English eat this no?" I just cried, Graham had to explain that I am very emotional at the moment due to pregnancy. The food was delightful and we asked if we could book into the bed and breakfast for the rest of the week. The owner kindly told us that they are fully booked and that nowhere will have any rooms as it is the French Bank Holiday this weekend. I looked at Graham (he looked as white as a ghost) and panicked as we had not booked anywhere else as we wanted to see what this place was like first, great, after tomorrow we are stranded in France and I am nearly 30 weeks pregnant. Guess what? I cried again.

New Day

We went out for a walk in France early evening and it was so lovely, we settled on a really sweet looking restaurant that was very busy and the food smelt divine. We were shown to a table outside by the fountain they had, and we ordered straight away as we were so hungry. I ordered the duck. When it came out I was so gutted I couldn't eat it as it was rare as in not cooked at all, so Graham said he would have it. I couldn't wait for my main because at this point I was soooo hungry and I ordered the beef medium to well done. When it arrived it was bloody raw mince so I couldn't eat that, so Graham explained why to the waiter so they then came out with a cheese dish but I couldn't eat that either as it was all the soft cheeses. So in the end I just said I would have the sugared crepes. What can go wrong with them? Well, I wish I hadn't bothered as they tasted like they had been cooked 6 times over and had a hint of a car tyre taste. Guess what? I bloody well cried. So on the way back we stumbled across a little crepe house and we went inside and I stuffed my face with the tastiest crepes I have ever tasted.

New Day

On our way home now and I can't believe this is going to be our last holiday on our own as husband and wife. We are going to be a mummy and daddy in 10 weeks, OH MY GOD IM GOING TO BE A MUM. I can't be a mum-I am only 30 and I haven't grown up yet. It is going to really hurt, oh my god it's going to really hurt. I think I need to sit down as I think I am having a panic attack.

New Day

So my 1st book New Day is going ok, it's not making me rich but it is helping me buy things for baby. It is a tough world out there.

WEEK 30

I got caught looking on the internet for prams and baby furniture at work today. I think they realise that I am not into my job now! I must admit it has become very boring now as I am on light duties, and at around 2pm I am so tired I need a nap, so I kind of just zone out!

New Day

My midwife has made me some appointments with the physio at the local hospital for my hips and back, and today was my first session to sort out this pubic pelvis thing I have developed. I got taken into this room which you could hardly swing a cat in (why you would ever do that is beyond me)? All it had in there was a weighing machine and a bed which took up all the room, so you can imagine, me a large pregnant woman and a VERY large Physio in there made it a tad cosy!

She told me to strip off to my knickers which got me all hot and flustered as it was so bloody small and awkward for me. When I turned round to face her she pulled out this object that looked like a large sex toy (not that I know what a large sex toy looks like) and said "lie down and relax and let me know where it hurts". So I did. I just laid down, I didn't even ask where she was thinking of sticking this thing, then Oh My God mmmmmmm this is sooooooo good. It turned out this object was a massaging rod with balls for my back. It was the best massage I have had in a long time. I told her not to stop as it is relaxing me and she carried on for 45minutes. (I fell asleep and woke up with dribble on the pillow). When I was getting changed I was hoisting my boobs into my bra (it's like an eagles nest it is so big), I looked up and realised that the window I had been doing this at had no curtains, no blinds and no privacy glass and saw that across the block was an old man holding his piss bag staring at me. I cried.

New Day

I shaved my lady bits today whilst I still can. Graham said it was looking like a coconut last night so I thought I'd better sort it before bump covers it. Whilst I was in the bathroom happily shaving away with an electric razor it suddenly dawned on me that Jack my stepson was roaming around the flat to and from the lounge. When I appeared from the bathroom he looked at me oddly, I was mortified. He must have thought I was using a different kind of electronic vibrating thing so I made such a big thing about how noisy razors are these days and how fab my legs look now they have been done. (When I looked down I had realised that they had not been done because I was shaving my bits not my legs, so I have just made it look even worse). I just went into my bedroom and stayed there until Jack went out. That night Graham went under the covers and I thought my luck was in, but no, he was going under the covers to talk to bump!

New Day

We went into the new John Lewis store that has just opened, we love it there as this is where we buy lots of stuff for our home. Anyway, we thought we would check out the baby section to get a buggy. I can't remember the name of this one buggy they had but it was £750 and I instantly fell in love with it. Graham asked the assistant what the hell it did for that sort of money and the assistant said "it has shock absorbers" Graham then said "it should have a dump valve, turbo, indicators, dvd player and sunroof at that sort of price" so we decided to settle for the Mclarens at £260 which was basically the same. Graham liked this one as it is black and lime green, he refused to get a pink buggy as he said it's not a good look for men!

New Day

I have a day off today to go to our antenatal class, I am so excited and so is Graham. When we got there Graham started looking so nervous, in fact all the dads did. There are some right characters here, I'm really shocked seeing how different the partners are from each other. For instance there was a lady who looked about 17 who was with a man of about 50 (I know they are together as I hear them telling another couple they had been married 3 months). There was a really stunning lady with what I would describe as an undernourished rat. I wonder if people are looking at Graham and I saying things about us? Oh my god- the woman who was doing the whole talk on how to breathe during birth, how to bath baby, how to wind baby, how to breast feed baby and all the other stuff you need to know was like an over excited Davina McCall with a bit of me, and that's border line scary.

The most scariest of the ladies was the lady showing us breach birth using a plastic womb and baby, she told us that she does not have children but she is in love with this doll and it makes her broody. She started talking baby talk to it for about 2 minutes whilst we all sat there looking awkward at each other, Graham excused himself to go to the loo and so did 2 other dads to be. So when the tea break came (this course was 9am until 5pm not my idea of a day off) everyone sat in almost silence (Graham said it was because we were all slightly stunned by the mad woman's actions). I can't understand how a woman who has never experienced child birth can teach you about pain relief and what the feeling is like, they may as well have had a man teaching it.

New Day

Graham and I went swimming today to relax my hips and legs because they have been giving me a bit of jip and the physio said it would be good for the pain. Anyway after my swim I was getting dressed in the changing rooms when some woman who was naked decided to make a beeline for me out of all the people in there. She started a conversation with me about the temperature of the pool and how she complains as it is always cold. I didn't know where to look either at her long door draft excluder boobs or her 1970's hairy muff! When I finally escaped,

Graham looked so happy to see me, he thought I had gone into labour in there as I took so long.

WEEK 31

I phoned in to work sick again, (my new nickname is sick note). I have the flu and I can't move, the worst thing about it is I am not allowed any medication because I am pregnant. So I have to lie here all day in bed. Graham has had to go to work so he has left me a flask of decaf tea and some ginger biscuits. My neighbour had baked me a dirty fat lemon cake that was so tasty and my other neighbour who lives below me bought me up all my trashy magazines (she knows me so well, I have only known her properly for about 2 years but she is like a sister I can tell all my worries to. I must tell her how much I appreciate our friendship). I could get used to this. I think I was a princess in my former life, as I am very good at barking orders and getting things done for me.

New Day

I called my mum today to ask her if it was normal to feel like I am having a heart attack and burping up what I can only describe as acid (my heartburn is back). "It's ok" my mum said "it is perfectly normal".

New Day

I can't bloody sleep at the moment. I go to sleep about 7pm and wake up at 1am and then I am wide awake. So I googled this as it was something I didn't want to worry my doctor or midwife about. Apparently this is normal for 31 weeks and I am not to have exercise or caffeine before bed (well this is worrying because I don't do any exercise and I don't have caffeine, I have decaf), so I am going to try milky drinks and warm baths to settle me. Graham said that I should try to go to bed later because he would get to see more of me and I might sleep through longer. I do feel bad as I see Graham for about 1 hour when he gets home and then I go to bed, I have so much making up to do.

New Day

I am getting so fed up with people asking me "how are you feeling today?" like I am dying. They never gave a toss before I was pregnant, so why give a toss now? I know they are just being nice and I know I will miss it when I have had bubba but it does get a little annoying.

New Day

We went to one of my best friends 30th at a social club near them and I absolutely loved it. It was like being on EastEnders. Everyone knew each other, everyone was chatting, dancing and having a laugh. I was just hoping nothing would kick off! I got to wear my lovely full length black fitted dress, new shoes, and my favourite bag from Cloudberry Bags. I had my hair done, my nails done, did my makeup really nice and felt a million dollars. So many people said I looked so fresh and that I was blooming with my tidy little neat bump. Graham even said that I had a sexy wiggle going on (I didn't have the heart to tell him that I wasn't doing a sexy wiggle, it's just when I walked, my thong was itching my pile and it felt good if I wiggled more when I walked).

WEEK 32

I called my mum today to see if it was normal that my belly button was full on popping out of my tummy? Mum said that this is fine, it's completely normal.

New day

I only just made it into work today as I'm really struggling to fit in the car and my hips bloody hurt. I bet this is what it is like to be old My midwife told me to get my bag packed and ready just in case, I told her that I had already done this at 25 weeks pregnant as I am so organised and bloody excited. It just hit me again that oh my goodness I am going to be a mum, and I have to give birth, and now I am really scared not excited. Oh my god, oh my god, oh my god, I need to call my mum. She said it's normal to panic!

New Day

I was so embarrassed today at work. I was making everyone tea and I sneezed 4 times in a row and wet myself a little bit, so I panicked and threw a cup of water over me to disguise it. A few of the ladies in the office were concerned as I looked tired and shaken from the water accident and sent me home. I am not sure who cleaned up my wee disguised as a puddle of water. I hope it was Michael the office idiot.

New Day

I swear my belly keeps getting tighter and it hurts a bit. Well it is uncomfortable, so Graham came home and timed the tightening and they were every 15 minutes and my belly shape changed every time. Graham called the midwife who came out straight away. She said I am fine and that these are in fact Braxton Hicks which are very normal, and that I would KNOW when I am having real contractions (the way she said this haunted me a little).

WEEK 33

Ok so I am the size of a house, overnight I must have put on around a stone, so altogether I have put on about 3 stone. I made the mistake of getting on the scales. It is official, Jane has hit the 12 stone 8 pounds mark on the scales! I have never seen the scales go over 10 stone 8 pounds (this is a lie as I once went to weight watchers as I went over 11 stone at the age of 21 as I found the taste for Beer). I cried and cried and Graham told me to stop crying as most of the weight will be baby and fluid. So I googled at 33 weeks to see how much the baby should weigh and it said 3 to 4 lbs........... Shit.

New Day

I swear I need to have our baby now, I don't think my body can stretch anymore (still no stretch marks, apart from the ones under my boobs which are looking really bad). I just feel really heavy and uncomfortable, I find it so hard to walk anywhere as I get so tired, so quickly. I really can't be bothered to go to work today it's so boring. I hate it, I just want to stay home and be in bed snuggling Graham.

New Day

Ok so today my hands looked rather puffy and Graham poked my feet which left a dent made from his thumb stay there for a while, so I called my mum to see if this was normal "it's not normal" so I put the phone down and panicked. I got on the internet and I've diagnosed myself with pre-eclampsia, great so now baby and I are in danger. Graham called the midwife and she came out straight away. She gave me a once over and said it is just fluid and baby and I are fine.

New Day

I called the midwife out again today as I have diagnosed myself with obstetric cholestasis which is when you get itchy hands, soles of your feet and tummy (I only have an itchy tummy, but 1 out of 3 is good enough for me to worry). My midwife said that I am fine and it's just where my skin is stretching to fit baby in whilst she is growing and I was told to keep rubbing the oil all over me. My midwife dropped a bombshell on Graham and I today and told us that she is going on a cruise when our baby is due, but not to panic as only 3% of women give birth on their due date! So I now panic and tell Graham that I can't give birth anymore as I need this woman here with me. Graham told me to stop being dramatic and that the chances of actually having our midwife there anyway would only be a 40% chance. "Well I think you should bloody well change your holiday, customers are always right" I cried. Graham turned bright red and told me to stop being so rude and turned to the midwife and apologised and the midwife just looked at me like I was an ogre!

WEEK 34

Shit I have 6 weeks left until I am a mum! Now that is scary! Everyone at work is getting bored of me as apparently all I do is moan! Well to be fair to me I am not surprised as I have so many reasons to always moan.

- I hate work
- I hate most of the people there
- I have to go to the loo every 20 minutes
- My hips are broken (well they might as well be)
- I am now struggling to drive
- I am fat
- I am either always to hot or too cold, never just right
- I keep getting cramp
- I keep puffing up like a bullfrog
- I get about 4 hours sleep at night and I am knackered
- None of my clothes fit anymore

So, no I am not surprised looking at that list why I am always bloody moaning.

New Day

I was so scared today I couldn't feel baby moving much, so Graham called the midwife who told us to go to the ward for a scan to check all was ok. I did call my mum beforehand and asked if it is normal and she said it isn't so I am now thinking the worst.

We got to the hospital and had to wait for about an hour to be seen. Graham was going nuts because all he could think about was our baby in distress. Finally we were called in and I was strapped up to all sorts of machines and had a scan. Baby is all ok. The doctor just said that there is not much room in there anymore which means baby won't be somersaulting as much. We were there for 5 and a half hours, poor Graham.

New Day

I fell asleep at work today. I went down to the lunch room and sat on the sofa and that was me gone. The next minute I knew Scott came down and woke me with a cuppa, laughing at me as I had been asleep and snoring for about an hour and a half.

New Day

Ok, so I went to the doctors again as I am like a puffer fish and the doctor said I need to slow down, so my boss has said I can work from home! Whoop Whoop what a bonus, I am so so so so happy. Everyone at work hates me now because I have escaped the hell hole.

New Day

Oh my god I am going to be a mum. I just keep crying today I am so scared, I have not told anyone that I am scared, I just say I am fine and that it is not bothering me but I am so frightened. My body has changed from toned, beach goddess, happy go lucky woman to an overweight, big breasted, waddling emotional wreck with piles, wonky hips and having to wear Tena pads and I am only 30 years old. How any woman says they love being pregnant is beyond me.

WEEK 35

I have had the worst night ever, Graham is cheating on me again in my dreams and I keep dreaming our baby is born a bear. This is what it must be like taking drugs. My midwife told me that baby can see light shining onto my belly and will turn her head towards it, so all day and into the evening I have been putting a torch to my belly.

New Day

I went to breakfast with my best friend Sarah today and as we walked passed a group of scaffolders, one of them shouted a crude comment then realised I was heavily pregnant, and one of them said "cor look, it is actually 3 of them, we are well in there". We both cringed and just carried on walking. They should be locked up. I bet their wives and girlfriends are proud of them.

New Day

Graham said I am waddling like a penguin now. I punched him, hard.

New Day

I feel like I could run a marathon today, I've so much energy, but my pelvis hurts a lot. This brace I'm wearing to help me walk is crap, it does nothing apart from leave indents on me.

I went for a stroll along the beach for about an hour, I got home around 1pm and Graham came home to find me asleep amongst the hoover, duster and magazines it was now 5pm!

New Day

Graham had booked a table for us at Goodwood Kennels restaurant tonight. I am so excited it is one of my favourite places to eat. We got all dressed up and when we got there I ordered a starter and it was delightful. I then ordered my main and I could only eat 3 mouthfuls, I was full up. I just burst into tears and the waiter was so lovely he asked if everything was ok. I explained that my baby has taken up all my room in my belly and I can't eat anymore, he went off for a moment and came back with a complimentary decaf coffee and a beautiful bowl of ice cream. I was happy after this and baby enjoyed the ice cream.

New Day

We have had to move into mum and dads again as the roof in our flat is leaking and the builders are fixing it so we have a home to bring baby back to. They said it will take 2 weeks to fix the problem so I hope mum and dad don't mind that we are going to take over their house again. Mind you, now I am working from home, I can cook all the dinners to save my mum having to always do it.

WEEK 36

Ok so I am 30 years old and I am wearing Tena Pads regularly because every time I sneeze or cough I wee a little, what the bloody hell is that all about? I remember saying to my friends "shoot me when I have to wear Tena Pads" I was expecting to be wearing them when I was in my 80's not my 30's. The other thing I noticed was, after I finished going for a wee, I stand up and then I start to wee again. I am so worried, I called my mum to see if it was normal. "It's normal".

New Day

I have had my 36 week check up with my midwife and my blood pressure is high, I have glucose in my wee and she thinks baby is breech. I have got to go to hospital for a scan now to see if this is the case. I may have to have baby in 2 weeks? We are not even in our own home, this can't happen, I can't be a mum yet, I am not ready.

New Day

I have been getting a few cramp like feelings today but I think it is Braxton Hicks. I don't want to alarm anyone, so I am kind of keeping it to myself. I don't want Graham thinking I am a wimp, but if I am totally honest I am so bloody scared. I can't believe I have got to push a child out of my moomin. My baby should be around 49cm now, so I am worrying myself that if I go full term my baby is going to be about the size of a cruise liner and weigh about the same as a cruise liner. I am struggling to go for a poo some days and now I have got to push a baby out. Oh shit, oh shit, oh shit, why did I agree to this, there must be an easier way surely? I mean, we apparently stretch and our bodies are amazing, but shit I do not know how I am going to pass something the size of a watermelon out of something the size of a cherry. Ouch, Ouch, OUCH.

New Day

I have been looking at drugs to take when I am in labour and giving birth. I keep saying a water birth but I am now thinking epidural, diamorphine, gas and air the lot. I have never taken drugs so I might as well take what I can without getting arrested, experience being high, and then on my come down I will be as high as a kite from meeting our new baby.

WEEK 37

Reflecting back on the day, I think I have upset my mum because, since moving in I have been fussing. For example, I emptied all her cupboards and told her to throw loads of stuff out. "Do you need this? Do you need that?" My mum looked a little upset or pissed off, not sure which. I also turned all the tins of food so they were facing out, I seem to have caught a bit of OCD or I am starting to nest.

New Day

My midwife weighed me today, I have put on 3 stone! I broke down and cried, she reassured me that a lot of this will be fluid. Fingers crossed that this is the case, Graham said that my boobs must weigh at least a stone each! I can breathe so much better today now the baby has dropped. I can now finish all my meals without leaving any on my plate. I feel so great so this week that I am going to stuff my face with all sorts of food another stone won't harm me! I am finding it hard to walk at the moment though as baby is well wedged down, so I am struggling quite a bit. I also think I need a better brace as this one is not supporting my hips enough. Midwife said baby weighs around 6 and a half pounds now (shit so this means that 2 stone 8lbs is just fluid, I am going to burst like a collapsing dam). My midwife also said to me I may start to feel anxious and worry about giving birth but everything will be just fine. I told her that I have been worrying since the day I found out I was pregnant.

New Day

We have had severe weather over night and today everywhere is flooded and to make matters worse I have been having pains all through the night and this morning they were 10 minutes apart. My mum suggested we called the midwife, who sent us to hospital. It took us nearly 1 hour to get there as the roads are under water, it should have only taken 20 minutes. Once we arrived things started to feel very, very real and I started to panic. I had to get dressed into a gown and was strapped up to machines with 1 blue and 1 pink band around my tummy. They are contractions but they think it is just Braxton Hicks. They are concerned though, as baby's heart rate has dropped so I have got to stay in overnight to keep an eye on us, in case I have to have an emergency C-section (by this time I am hysterical). I kept crying "we're not ready, we don't have a home to go back to yet, I am too young, I can't do this" (I am going to be a nightmare when I do give birth I know I am, I am a wimp). Graham calmed me down and then went outside to call my mum and dad to let them know. They started to panic also, but Graham soon calmed them and told them it was fine, and if anything happens he will call them straight away. It got to 8.30pm Graham kissed and hugged me and bump, said his goodbyes and left.... I have never felt so lonely.

I was on a ward with 6 other women, I found out that one of them was due a c section in the morning as baby had no room left and was struggling a bit. The midwife asked her if this was her 1st and the woman said "no my 5th" the midwife nearly choked and so did all of us women. She looked scared even though she has done this 4 times already. It has been raining all day and it's now 11.30pm and it is still pouring with rain. The midwife came in to say it is flooded really bad and we won't be going anywhere unless we have a boat, turned the lights out and told us to rest. I kept texting Graham but he must have fallen asleep around midnight as I had no reply. At around 3am the fire alarms filled the wards and we all just laid there and then after about 3 minutes one of the women said "do we just lie here and burn or do we try and get out?" We all burst into laughter (makes a change for me) as we all had no idea what we were supposed to do. The midwife came into our ward and told us not to panic, the alarms have gone off because the ground floor of the hospital has been flooded, and we have had a month's worth of rain in 3 hours. When the alarms stopped, it was silent and then out of nowhere we all heard mooing, groaning and screaming it went on for about 45 minutes so I just laid there thinking shit she is giving birth and I am going to have to do that soon. When it finished the woman opposite me said "Shit, did you just hear that, that is what we will be experiencing soon" I didn't sleep well after that. I texted Graham to see how everything was, and he told me that our house we rent out to a family has flooded, and the roof has caved in, and the flat we are having fixed ready for baby has got worse. All the rain has lifted whatever they had put down to sort out the old problem, so it will take an extra week now. I just cried myself to sleep and told baby to hang on, I want our home to be perfect for her.

New Day

I have been released from hospital yay. When I got home all my friends were there waiting for me for my baby shower, it was such a lovely surprise. Bump and I were spoilt rotten. I didn't realise what a bitch fest baby showers are, we just gossiped about everyone and anything. Loads of photos were taken so I can put them in an album for baby to see when she grows up.

New Day

Only a couple of days until I bugger off on maternity leave, I can't wait. I kindly called Lara, Scott and Michael to tell them that I shall be going soon. Lara told me to "shut up" and can't wait to do the same. Scott said he wished he was a woman and Michael was his usual prick of himself, I hope he gets the sack before I return!

WEEK 38

Graham has just told me that part of him does not want to be at the birth, I am now full of mixed emotions about this. I understand that he is scared, but he is my rock and I need him, I am the one that is scared!

New Day

I spoke to our baby last night and told her to hurry up. I am fed up being fat, tired and immobile. She high fived me which made me cry. I can't wait to hold her. I can't stop wondering how different our lives are going to be. Graham has said it will change everything and that it will shock me at how much you realised you did do! I wonder who she will look like?

New Day

Graham has said that he does not want any more children as he does not like seeing me so poorly (we haven't even had this child yet) I have had a bit of a bad time though from the start, being sick most days, not being able to walk properly, emotions making my blood pressure hit the roof and so on. I am not sure if he actually means it or that what he actually means is he doesn't like me getting fat and walking around like an elephant that just swears and cries all day every day!

New Day

I asked Sarah my best friend when is the best time to get an epidural, she replied "as soon as you find out your pregnant". I also asked her what it meant when the baby's head is crowning and she said "not only does it feel like a crown is coming out of you, it also feels like the entire throne is trying to come out". I did laugh, but I'm now even more bloody scared than I was this morning.

New Day

My midwife told me that women experience diarrhoea now as the body is getting ready for the birth, so if I get this don't be alarmed, only be alarmed if it happens a lot! So not only am I now fat, sweaty and hairy I am now going to shit myself! Apparently cleaning my back passage will make my baby's journey easier? I think they mean cleaner!

WEEK 39

Graham has a new name for me and that is MOOMIN (Great, I call my lady bits this)! That's a nice way of saying I look like a fat fucking Hippo, with a fat face, apparently this is not the case. Graham said I am like a cute hippo! Whatever....

Graham also said I swear a lot since becoming pregnant and I need to stop when baby is born! Whatever......

I have told him it is probably my hormones and that he needs to stop picking on me. To be fair to him though looking back through my diary, I have sworn a lot. Whatever......

New Day

We went into one of the DIY stores near us to choose some bits for the nursery and we have a card that gives you money off, but it should be called "what's the point card". Whenever we use it you either get no discount or it counteracts the offer that is already on the product and adds more to it, so it becomes more expensive. I threw it in the bin on the way out-bloody useless.

New Day

I know 9 women in my circle of friends that have had their babies already but mine however is still inside, I know I have 3 days until my due date but hurry up. I am fat, bloated, tired, breathless, sore, sweaty and looking ugly, in fact I feel like how half of the women look in the town I live in!

New Day

Count down! I can't sleep it is madness, I really am scared now I really have to do this. I have avoided everybody's texts and phone calls since yesterday, I think I will break down if I speak to anyone nice! I have been reading all the books again about how to give birth and found I couldn't concentrate so I googled women giving birth. I just sobbed it looks so painful, I am not ready for this. I called my mum to speak to her, she panicked as it was 7am and she thought I had gone into labour. I told her I was ok and that, no, bump is still not ready, just needed a hug over the phone as I am now scared.

WEEK 40

OH SHIT, OH FUCK, OH SHIT "Graham, I have wet myself and there is pink jelly in my knickers"

"Honey your waters have broken, and that pink jelly I think is called the show" (bloody hell, he really has been reading that book I got him).

"MOOOOOOOOOOOOOOOOOOOOOOOOOOOO HHHHHHHHHHHHHHH, MOOOOOOOOOOOOO, OHHHHHHHHHHHH ARGHHHHHHHHHHH, I want my mum"

"Oh god Jane, you ok, you sound like a cow in distress?"

"I am a fucking cow in distress, call the bloody midwife. MOOOOOOOOOOOOOO, HOOOOOOOOOOOOOO, OHHHHHHHHHHHHHHHH, ARGHHHHHHHHHHHHHHH"

"She is on holiday and it is 1am"

"I DON'T CARE CALL HER"

"She is on holiday"

"BITCH, CALLLLLLLLLLL THEEEEEEEEEEEEEE MOOOOOOOOOOOOOOOOO OHHHHHHHHHHHHHHHHH HOSSSSSSSSSSSSPITALLLLLLLLLLLLLLLLLLLLL"

Graham called the hospital and they wanted to speak to me!

“Hello Jane, how are you?” (are they winding me up)

“I am giving birth, how the hell do you think I am?”

“Is this your first baby?”

“Yes and my LAST OHHHHHHHHHHHHHHHHHHHHHHHHH, MOOOOOOOOOOOOOOOOOO, OHHHHHHHHHHHHHHH”

“Take some Paracetamol Jane that will dull the pain”

“Paracetamol? I need to be put to sleep, it feels like a double decker bus is trying to pass out of my vagina”

“Right ok Jane, how often are the pains”

“every 10 minutes”

“ok, well Jane, you don’t need to come into the hospital until the pains are 6 minutes apart”

“so what am I suppOOOSSSSEDD TOOOOOOOOO DOOOOOOOOOOOOOOO, OHHHHHHHHHHHHHHH IT REALLY HURTSSSSSSSSSSSSSSSS, I WANT MY MUM”

“Have some paracetamol and call back when they are closer together”

I slammed the phone down and cursed her. Graham looked embarrassed and beside himself and I looked and sounded like I was dying. I wonder what the neighbours must think.

After 40 minutes Graham took me to the hospital it was 2.30am, apparently all I kept saying was “it’s falling out, she is falling out, help me, my baby is falling out" (how embarrassing for Graham).

When we arrived they put me on a hospital bed and the Doctor came round and said that he has to put his fingers inside me to feel how far I was into the labour, I kicked him full on in the face as it felt like his whole body had just entered me, apparently I was only 4cm gone and he sent me home. I cursed him.

We went back to my parents and I heard Graham telling them about how I assaulted the Doctor and how I was lucky they didn't press charges (I just hope he never has to have a Doctor inserting their hands up his bits). I was so glad to see my mum and dad, one because they are my life, and two, I needed Graham to be looked after as he doesn't look too good (it must be awful seeing your loved one in pain like this).

My mum put me in the bath and I cried, saying that I will not be having a water birth, it won't help and that I am scared, I am really, really scared.

My poor mum and dad had to watch their daughter in pain mooing like a cow, and poor Graham didn't know what to do as everytime he tried to rub my back and say it will be fine I just shouted (I think I may have been foaming at the mouth) "IS IT, IS IT GOING TO BE OK? IT FUCKING HURTS AND DON'T TOUCH ME", by 5am we were back in the car on the way to hospital as I was in so much pain. The women that told me it feels like a period pain but 10 times worse-you're all bloody liars, it feels like the titanic is trying to push out of my vagina!

We arrived at the hospital and Graham dropped me off outside so he could park (otherwise he would get clamped, it is so wrong, I am giving birth for god sake there should be a drop off point). Whilst he was gone I collapsed in the entrance way crying in a heap as I couldn't stand up. I went to sit in a wheel chair but you have to pay £1 to use it (like the trolleys at the supermarkets bloody cheek). I was so lucky a nurse found me who was just coming on duty and put a pound in for me and waited with me until Graham came back.

We all got in the lift and went to the ward, I was checked out and was 6cm, oh my god how am I going to cope I have to go another 4cm. I am now making so much noise that they insert a needle full of diamorphine into me. We got put in a room with another couple who were also going to become parents shortly. She was panting, rocking side to side like she was making a fitness dvd. I looked over at her and slurred "what an earth are you doing?" she said "I am going all natural, no drugs just me and my lungs" I just burst out laughing (I am off my head by this point as the drugs have kicked in) and said "What a waste you can take any drugs you want to, not feel anything and you won't get arrested, I love this bed and this room I am going to live here, oh I need a cup of tea, am I having a baby, I look fat?" I then fell asleep. Apparently Graham said it was the best thing that could have happened as the couple looked scared and he was really embarrassed as I didn't even know what I was saying or doing, he just said I was completely off the wall.

About an hour and a half later I woke up screaming "SHE'S FALLING OUT, I AM GOING TO PUSH, OOOOOOOOOOOOOOOOOOOOOOOOOOOOO OO MOOOOOOOOOOOOOOOOOOOO OHHHHHHHHHHHHHHHHHHHHHHHHHHHHHMOO OOOOOOOOOOOOOOOOOOOOOOOOOOOOO OOOOOHHHHHHHHHH" The nurse came in and said that I was only 8cm, I said I didn't give a shit, and carried on.

The next bit is a blur and Graham filled me in, he said that I was pushing for 2hours and 45mins and in between contractions I was Jekyll and Hyde, and that I was unconscious in between each push. The midwife wouldn't allow me to have an epidural as I was too far into my labour, and that when he tried talking to me, it took him back to when I was drunk at a festival I met him at (oh great so I looked like I was giving birth that night-I thought I looked hot)! He also told me he broke down half way as he hated seeing me in pain, and had to leave me for a few minutes to compose himself. (This still makes me want to cry when I think of this, as I can't imagine how lonely and scary it is for the men to see their wives go through all this pain).

The part I remember is when the midwife said "I can see her head, do you want to touch it?" I think I then fainted at the thought! I pushed and pushed and all I can say is that it feels lovely pushing as it stops the pain of the contractions (contractions are by far the most painful part of pregnancy). It feels a lot like you are trying to poo out a tree, the pressure on your backside is massive (I think I may have had an accident but I will never know as she was very clean this midwife, always changing the sheets). Any way

Graham was now in control holding my leg up to the side watching our baby popping in and popping out, He seriously was my rock, he was helping me to breathe and calm myself down. When all of a sudden I pictured the dinosaur in Jurassic park when it is running in the kitchen straight at the people and then the midwife saying “stop pushing and pant” and me just screaming “SHESSSSSSSSSSSSSSSS FALLLLLLENNNNNNNNNNNNNN OUTTTTTTTTTTTTTTTTTTTTTTT” and there she was, my beautiful baby girl, our beautiful baby girl.

A few words of advice from my work friends when I asked "what advice can you give me now I am pregnant?"

- Good luck!!!

- Don't do it!!!

- Make sure that when she does eventually leave home that she STAYS away!!

- My only advice, albeit as a dad, is make time for plenty of golf in between changing nappies. And get your partner to do the rest.......You ignored the advice I gave u in the past, but I will try again. So listen very carefully. Fist have an affair with a short fat middle aged man called Me, fleece your husband and then set me up in a love nest. And last but not least, get a good price when you sell your brood to the sex trade

- Make sure you have vasaline when you give birth. You'll need it for your first pee.

- Enjoy the time off xx

- All the very best; enjoy your last few weeks of independence.

- It's too late for my tips.......you've already done it! Lol

- Enjoy your little angel, they grow up too fast - seriously.

- Don't be surprised in about 12 years when she turns into a demon, where even eye contact either launches in to a mega strop or floods of tears. From experience this is not a passing fad, and I can personally vouch for it lasting in excess of three years

- Learn the language, 'yeah', 'like', 'OMG' are key, and probably the only three words they will use. Anything else will be an incomprehensible murmur. If they do ever talk to you, they're after new clothes. Accept that an area of your house will look like a hangover from the Bosnian crisis. Lastly, and most importantly, **NEVER** buy them a contract phone. Their inability to converse with you is not replicated with the remainder of the world who they will happily talk to for hours, all to the extreme pleasure of Vodafone!

- I don't have much experience with babies, only dogs so I'm not sure my tips would be of any use!!!

- I hope it all goes well for you, take some tablets as I've heard it might sting a bit

- Tell your other half to relax and breathe deeply that will help him. Don't hold any part of his body when you are having contractions, you will either kill him or the part you're holding will come off in your hand

- Take loads of photos, keep a diary of your thoughts and the changes to your baby

- Try not to worry, relax and be happy

- Your child will drive you mental, my boys did that to me, but they are brilliant so it is worth it

- I don't need to wish you luck because you're going to be great! And you'll be in and out of hospital in an afternoon with that beautiful baby!

- Good luck, after the problems you had initially with the pregnancy, actually giving birth will be a breeze, and if all else fails a really good excuse for a swear!!! You'll do brilliantly and be a super mum, I fully expect to see your little girl totally co-ordinated and wearing the latest shoes!

- It's been great knowing you over the past four years and thanks for all your help and support.

- It's going to be so strange for you to be a Mum. Everyone says your priorities change and your outlook on life completely alters when you have a baby – I think you'll be a great Mum.

- I'm sure motherhood will be stressful, but just enjoy it and make the most of moulding a new person into the world. I wonder what your child will be doing in 25 years from now!! Weird.

My 1st interview with Cloudberry Bags

www.cloudberrybags.co.uk

Tell us about yourself

My name is Emma Gibbens, I am married to Mark and we have a Daughter who is 2 going on 12 and son who is 20 (I am the wicked step mother).

We live in a little cottage in the middle of nowhere, which is good as I tend to talk a lot and quite loudly. (Sorry for those who know me, I have tried very hard to not talk as much and to be quieter but I have found this impossible so we just thought it would be best to move).

We have a cat called Rambo but he lives with my parents after our daughter was born, he loves it there and now ignores me (he needs to remember I pay his pet insurance).

We are quite an active family we are always up to something, we love surfing, walking, reading, nature, theatre, swimming and travel around to different National Trust properties. I get a lot of my writing ideas when we visit new places.

Outline of your day to day life

I really don't know how I have written a book, I am a director of our company Look Design & Build, I am an Author, I am a mother and a full time wife (that's the hardest part)! My husband will say that I spend too much time on the laptop when I am home from work but this is when I write my books. I am also on Twitter quite a lot in the evenings but this is my time to network and just be nosey!

My day is started by my daughter lifting up one of my eyelids saying "milky's mummy" this is around 6.30am. We all then go down for breakfast, then it's all a blur from there until bedtime.

How important is your handbag to you?

My handbag is like another limb of my body so I need one to be reliable, looking good, strong, medium sized/large (I sound like I am writing a dating add)!

How often do you change your everyday handbag?

I have around 20 bags all sorts of shapes and sizes, and my collection is now growing thanks to Cloudberry Bags (my husband has given up telling me I only need one bag).

I need a big bag for my paperwork, journals, books and laptop to fit in, but at weekends I like to have a smaller one because I usually end up carrying my daughter around (with her and a big bag it would be like carrying the weight of a small car).

What's in your handbag now?

I was dreading this question (please don't judge me). I have emptied my bag with a look of disgust from my husband. I have 1 laptop, 2 nappy sacks, a spare pair of my daughters clothes and knickers (she is potty training), post it notes, journal, 5 pens, 2 dongles, lip stick, lip gloss, glasses, 7 contact lenses, Peppa Pig toy (not mine), a book, a spoon, a sock (one of mine), 2 phones, looks like half a pack of crushed carrot type crisps, nail varnish, purse, photos, flat shoes (I wear heels a lot and sometimes I get blisters), plasters, a paperclip, tweezers, magazine, bottle of water, teabags, a plastic tomato, a plastic egg and a sponge (I think half of this stuff Beatrix has put in there).

I hear you all laughing at me and probably picturing me with wonky shoulders and walking like some troll that lives under a bridge (hey this could make a good book) due to the weight of my bag, but I promise it's not that heavy once you get used to it.

Is there a book in your bag?

Yes I am reading "Return to sender" by Zoe Barnes and it is very good, I also have my 1st draft of my second book "Pregnancy and Piles" which is bloody hilarious and is out November time.

If there's an iPod (or phone) with music on, what's your current favourite to listen to?

Now I can't believe I am admitting this, but I own a Samsung note 2 and I have had it for over a year, and still I don't know how to down load music on it so the answer to that question is there is nothing on my phone. But I know how to listen to the radio on there and I am usually listening to Capital fm or Spirit fm.

Who's style do you admire and why?

I love Kate Middletons style because it's so classic and never goes out of fashion, and I love Jennifer Anniston's style-it's just simple and effortless but looks amazing.

Have you any dreams you would like to achieve?

It was to become an Author and I have achieved this and I am so proud that I have done it, so my other dream is to build our dream home on the perfect plot of land.

And finally if you could choose one of Cloudberrys Bags, which would you choose and why?

I already have two and I use the Orange Knightsbridge most due to the size, I have now discovered the Tweed Essentials designs and this will be my next purchase now I am in the country side ;)

The Author of Matches Carlie Pettit Interviews Emma Gibbens the Author of New Day and Pregnancy & piles.

Books are escapism. Do you create worlds that you wish you lived in?

No not really I morph worlds from people I have met and what I have experienced. If I created worlds I wish I lived in my books would end up being princess comics!!!

Do you base characters on people you know, or would want to know?

Yes to both, some of my favourite characters are based on people I have overheard in a café or when at the gym and I am such a people watcher (not a stalker) and I create this world that they would live in then base my character on that.

What genre do you write?

What draws you to this genre? My first three books are humour/diaries/chic lit I love this style of writing because it is fun, and I love sarcasm and making people laugh. My first Novel is based in 1940 and has a bit of a fifty shades feel to it. I was drawn to this as I wanted to try a different style that has not been released yet, and I am still playing around with it.

What book do you wish you could have written?

A book on geography because I am crap with where places are (I thought that the spaghetti junction was in Italy, then was told by my mortified husband it is in fact in Birmingham)

What are you currently working on?

I am working on my 3rd book of the 3 diaries. The main characters are Jane and Graham who are newly married going through the phases of a new baby.... Very very funny, you will relate to it regardless if you have children or not. They are special because they are based on myself and husband (although a lot has been added which has not really happened, this is where you decide what is true!)

Quick Fire Questions

Dream Holiday?

A month in the thick of winter with my little family and I with my books, wine and lots of food, a massive inglenook fire in a cottage up in the Highlands. No phones, no computers, just us.

Worst Vice?

Brie

Tea or coffee?

Red Bush Tea/ latte-I can't chose

Crisps or Chocolate?

Crisps

What do you hate most about people?

Rudeness and liars

What irritates you?

People eating pears next to me, I hate slurping sound.

What makes you happy?

Seeing my family and friends happy.

These blank pages are for you to add your memories

of your 40 weeks ☺